Lie Kill Walk Away

MATT DICKINSON

ALSO BY
MATT DICKINSON

North Face
The Everest Files
Mortal Chaos
Black Ice
The Death Zone

shrine
bell

www.shrinebell.com

Matt Dickinson

First published in 2016 by Shrine Bell, an imprint of Vertebrate Publishing.

Shrine Bell
Crescent House, 228 Psalter Lane, Sheffield S11 8UT, UK
www.shrinebell.com

This book is a work of fiction. The names, characters, places, events and
incidents are products of the author's imagination. Any resemblance to actual persons,
living or dead, or actual events is purely coincidental.

A CIP catalogue record for this book is available from the British Library.

ISBN 978-1-910240-86-1 (Paperback)
ISBN 978-1-910240-87-8 (eBook)

10 9 8 7 6 5 4 3 2 1

Cover illustration, design and typesetting by
Nathan Ryder – Vertebrate Publishing.

Shrine Bell and Vertebrate Publishing are committed
to printing on paper from sustainable sources.

MIX
Paper from
responsible sources
FSC www.fsc.org FSC® C018072

Printed and bound in Great Britain by Clays Ltd, St Ives plc.

FOR MY DAUGHTER
ARIADNA

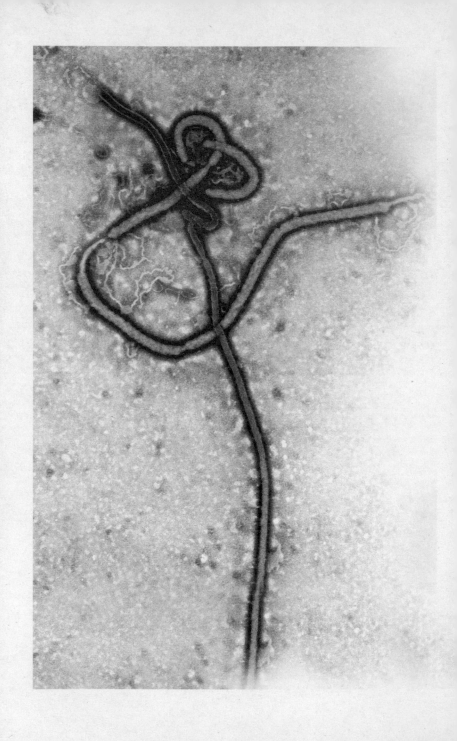

PART 1
INTO THE HOT ZONE

Patrick Eden: Biohazard suit sealed. I've got oxygen for fifteen minutes.

Police Command: Instructions from Defence HQ. Do not go in alone. I repeat: do not go in alone.

Patrick Eden: There's a man dying in there. I'm going in.

Audio transcript from helmet mic worn by Patrick Eden, UK Government bioweapons inspector following emergency call at SYMBARON lab, Hampshire.

Sleep shatters into a thousand ugly pieces. A distant scream worms its way into my waking mind.

'NO!'

I sit bolt upright in bed, my heart racing. A woman's cry. High pitched. Desperate. Down in the garden? Perhaps in the woods? It sounded like my mother.

But it can't be.

I take a few deep breaths, calming myself down and persuading myself it was just a nightmare. I swing my legs out from under the duvet and only then think to check the time.

Ten past nine.

I blink in surprise. It's way too late. During the summer holidays Dad wakes me at precisely eight o'clock with a cup of tea and two pieces of toast.

'Rebecca! Oh daughter mine! Get your lazy backside **out** of bed!' His morning serenade. Every single day of the holidays.

But not this one.

I slip off my nightdress and pull on jeans and a T-shirt. Something pricks my nostrils. I smell burned toast. I go to the top of the stairs and call down.

'Dad? Are you there?'

No reply. Something is wrong.

2 JOE FONTANA

It's a bit past midnight in north London. I've been spraying for fifteen minutes and this is how far I've got:

I'm working as fast as I can. Enjoying the mist. The jelly-baby fuzzy high that comes with it. Cans hissing away like silver serpents. Ears on radar alert for the crackle of a walkie-talkie. The wall belongs to some sort of military hospital so I'm on maximum alert.

There's not many people around, just a drunken old tramp in the park on the opposite side of the road. Way down the other end of the street there's a bunch of rowdies getting chucked out of a pub.

That's not my business.

Shamrock is with me. That's my dog. He's a daft, scruffy mutt but he's all right. I chose him from the shelter. On his sticker it said some kids had tied him up in a bin bag and thrown him in a canal for a laugh.

That's why I wanted him – show him people aren't all bad.

Now he's tied to a lamp post with a bit of string. Most taggers take dogs with them when they're spraying. Gives you an excuse to be out late on the streets.

'Just walking my dog, officer.' That sort of thing.

At the shadowy end of the street I see a dark car has stopped near the rowdy bunch.

Like I said, none of my business.

3 BECCA

Halfway down the stairs I see an envelope sitting on the doormat. I reach the hall and pick it up.

A Cambridge postmark; the name of the college printed in the top left-hand corner.

Oh. I feel my skin chill. My breath trips a tiny beat. There's no *way* that Dad would leave this envelope on the mat like that. Like it was junk mail or something.

It's my formal offer from Cambridge. A reward for the five A* A levels I scored just three days after my fifteenth birthday.

Mathematics. Biology. Physics. Chemistry. Applied Science.

This envelope means I'll be studying Natural Sciences, following in the footsteps of my dad. Some press people wanted to do an article about the fact I will be one of the youngest undergraduates ever, but I didn't want to make a fuss. I'd rather just get on with it.

Why didn't Dad pick the envelope up? It doesn't make sense.

Has he had another stress attack? The last few days have been unbearably hard for him. Life as a bioweapons expert was never going to be an easy ride.

Where has he gone? Maybe to the lab? I get a momentary surge of confidence: he will have left me a note somewhere. So I'd better take a look around and find it.

4 JOE

Still spraying. *Almost there*. Trouble is, the letters on this job are really big, so it's taking a bit of time.

Out of the corner of my eye I see that dark car is now moving up the street towards me. *Ignore it. Just ignore it*. I can't stop now – there's too much money riding on this job.

Yes. Cash. Fifty quid to get myself down here and spread the good word about Gary Barker. Whoever he is.

And I need that money to pay for a vet to get this nasty bump removed from Shammy's neck. I don't want to ask Dad for it because I know he's always skint. So I brought a beer crate to use as a stepladder, gave the two CCTV cameras a quick squirt of paint and I'm into the job.

I'm on the K now.

The car is still coming. Crawling down the road. Dead slow.

I shake the cans. I get back to the job. *Don't show fear. Stay calm*.

The car stops.

I turn as I hear the buzz of a window. Then I see there's three dodgy-looking men in there. And a woman as well. My heart hammers in my chest.

'Oi!' Her voice is hard as nails. 'D'you know what my name is?'

I shrug.

'Michelle Barker. Gary Barker's sister, as it happens.'

Ah. So now it *is* my business.

5 BECCA

I step along the hallway, heading for the library. It's the biggest room in the house, an old dining hall with a mock minstrels gallery and a huge stone fireplace.

I pause outside. 'Dad?'

Not a sound.

I push the door open, walking slowly into this most sacred room; a place where I have learned to be curious, to ask questions.

It was my choice to be home tutored. I wanted to stretch myself in a way no school could have done.

It's not just a matter of following in Dad's footsteps. It goes deeper than that. When I was eight, Dad was infected by Marburg fever – he was bitten by a chimpanzee in a test lab. I still remember the terror I felt as he was sealed in an isolation ward at the Hospital for Tropical Diseases in London.

Mum understood exactly what was happening: 'He's not alone,' she told me. 'He's got 250 billion white blood cells fighting tooth and nail to kill that virus.'

Her words helped me to keep hope alive. And those white blood cells did their job. Dad survived by the skin of his teeth and ever since then I had a secret and fierce ambition to learn about the ways these diseases work, to spend my life helping people survive the deadliest viruses on the planet.

The memory of that woman's cry floods back. I shiver to recall it.

Was it real? It couldn't be. *Could it?*

I leave the library and walk towards the office.

6 JOE

Now I'm well and truly gripped. Everything goes dead quiet for a few seconds. The men are giving me evils. Shamrock is growling.

Then the woman goes on: 'What's the big idea? Disrespecting my brother like that?'

I think about a reply. And here's the thing about me: if I get asked a question, I have this habit of blurting out a stupid answer even if I know it's going to get me deeper into trouble.

It's like my mouth gobs off and my brain's not in gear. Sometimes I even think it's funny. And that's why I say:

'It's nothing personal.'

There's a pause. Like when you press the button in a lift but nothing happens. And half a second can seem like a week. And the woman's eyes are bulging.

'You cheeky scumbag!' she screams. 'Grab him!'

The car doors fly open so fast it's like an explosion. I'm off the beer crate and it's clattering over as I snatch up my shoulder bag, cram in five or six of the cans.

I undo Shamrock's knot and *just* dodge the first outstretched arm. He's a big one, this man – bug eyed. Veins busting out on his forehead.

'Come on!' I tell Shammy. I grab his string and we start to run.

7 BECCA

I walk into the office. And the first thing I see is a photo frame lying on the floor. The glass is broken. Shards are scattered across the carpet. How has it fallen? I pick it up. A tiny splinter stabs my finger. A bright red drop of blood smears the silver frame.

My mother, Sarah. I know it sounds juvenile but sometimes I still think of her as 'Mummy'. Even though she is a stranger to me now.

The sense of loss has never left me. Even after 1,736 days. That's the type of mind I have, by the way. Ticking things off. Ordering. Filing things away in logical fashion.

'One day she will come back to us.' That's what Dad used to whisper as he tucked me into bed.

He doesn't say that any more.

I cross to his desk. A total train wreck. Everest-sized mounds of paper; an old pipe that he sucks on but never lights.

The chair is overturned. His mug of coffee is spilt. The creepy sensation of unease is morphing into a full-on dose of dread.

Where *is* he? What's going on?

I hit the space bar on the computer and the machine whirrs out of standby. On the screen I see the Google page of the day with the following words entered into the search box:

Ebola Anthrax Antigenic Shift

Then I see a tiny drop of blood on the floor. And this time it's not mine.

8 JOE

Faster! Run faster!

My heart's doing the jackhammer jive. Shammy's at my heels. The quickest of them just behind.

Right into the alley. Reeks real bad. The bag clunking against my ribs. Shamrock yelping and barking like mad.

I slip. Crash into a wheelie bin at high speed. Shammy dives for cover. Wind knocked. Lungs crushed.

'Run. Shammy!' I croak. But he just hides under the bin.

They pause to catch their breath. Then the biggest one's eyes spark up as he sees the bag of cans. 'What's your favourite colour, son?'

He looks at the name on the label.

'How about Tibetan Blue?'

I try to turn my head but his mates are stronger. I gasp in a few mouthfuls of air.

'Here you go.'

Then I get it. Right in the face. Then down my trousers. He's even squirting it into the holes of my ears. He's shaking those peas like his life depends on it and all I can hear is the hiss of the cans and the laughter.

I screw my eyes tight shut. Hold my breath. Try to protect my lungs.

And it goes on ... and on ... and on.

4 BECCA

I stare at the blood on the carpet. All of my senses heightened. It's been a roller-coaster week for Dad: he's gone from unknown scientist to notorious anti-government whistle-blower in one seismic shift.

Now what? Is he hurt?

I pull out my mobile, speed-dial his number. A phone rings out somewhere on the floor. I find it behind a fold of the curtain, next to the overturned chair.

'Dad?' I shout.

I enter the kitchen. There are two pieces of toast on the grill, both burned to a crisp although the gas is turned off. There is no note to be seen on the table and nothing pinned to the fridge.

Next to the kettle is a mug with an unused teabag in it. A herbal teabag; cinnamon and orange, the type of thing Mum used to drink.

The kettle is still warm.

I sense a powerful charge in the air. Like that feeling when you go into a theatre after the show has ended and the crowd has long gone. You can still feel the electricity of all those people; some of their energy has lingered.

I can feel that *something* has happened here. But I don't know what.

I must go outside. Look for him there.

I pour myself a glass of water. My hand is shaking as I drink.

10 JOE

Half a can of Tibetan Blue later and the three gents are getting tired of the fun.

'That'll teach you a bit of respect,' Sprayman says, and he gives me a final kick on the shin.

The can clatters into the wall. They head off into the night.

At first I'm puking. My eyes feel like I've been stung by wasps. I need to get some water on them but I can't move yet. I drag myself up. Can't even smell the stink of the alley any more. Just paint. Can't see much, it's like my eyelids are stuck together with superglue.

'All right, boy. You're OK.' I pull Shammy out from under the bins. I give him a pat on the head. He licks my hand. The poor mutt's whining like it was him who got the beating and not me.

Out of the alley. Get to the street. There's a few people here close to a pub.

'What's wrong with him?' some woman asks.

'Drunk student, I reckon,' says a voice. 'Probably painted his face blue for charity. Idiot.'

I decide to go back to the wall.

Dangerous? Yes, but I can't lose my other cans.

I'll just have to hope Gary Barker's sister and her friends aren't still hanging around.

11 BECCA

Outside. The air smells of dew-laden grass. Chilled water droplets prick between my toes.

The view from the garden normally fills me with pleasure; distant fields dotted with sheep and cattle, ancient pockets of woodland stretching as far as the eye can see. But today I have more important things on my mind.

'Dad!' Still no reply.

I decide to try the stables. I cross the little cobbled court-yard and push open the door.

Arcturus watches me with glittering eyes, his powerful body pressed into the deep shadows of the stall. On a normal day he radiates excitement when I call for him, wanting the speed and exhilaration of our morning race through the woods. Now his ears are pricked forward and I can see the tight prom-inence of the tendons in his neck – a sure sign of fear.

I raise my hand to him. But he shies away, iron-clad hooves skittering on the floor.

I return to the garden. At the bottom is the copse. Beech trees, alder, a few stately pines.

I walk slowly under the green canopy and breathe in the musty, decaying aroma of the leaf litter. Oddly, there's no bird noise at all. Just the rumble of a faraway aeroplane.

I take a few more steps. I don't even know what is compel-ling me to walk deeper into the copse.

And that's where I find him.

Hanging by the neck.

12 JOE

I reach the wall without any trouble. I'm still coughing, trying to rub the paint out of my eyes.

I get out my mobile and call the bloke who paid me to do the job. I tell him what's happened. And all he says is:

'Yeah, Gary's family live down the bottom of that road. That's why I chose that wall, mate – so he'd see it.'

'You could have warned me!'

'Did you finish it off? I'm not paying you unless ... '

I click off the phone. He's starting to annoy me.

Then – disaster. Just as I'm gathering up my stuff, a police car pulls up. No siren or nothing. It just cruises up quietly and this cop winds down the window.

'Bit late for you to be out on the streets isn't it, lad?'

The cop gets out of the car. And a second later his mate follows. They're putting on their hats in that way that lets you know they mean business.

'Come here in the light,' he says. I step towards him and him and his boy wonder start to laugh.

'Blimey! No need to ask you what your favourite colour is.'

It's difficult to reply. My tongue's starting to swell up.

'What are you doing out here at this time of night?'

I mumble, 'Just walking my dog, officer.'

13 BECCA

He looks like a puppet, his limbs dangling at odd angles; as if he's a scarecrow badly stuffed with straw. Dark globules of crimson blood are dripping from his left wrist where an ugly, jagged wound has ripped into his flesh.

A garden chair lies on its side just a few feet away. Next to it are his glasses, and a small penknife.

The scene looks unreal, like a movie set. I stand motionless. For a few seconds I am like a zombie as I stare dumbly up into my father's horribly contorted face.

Get an ambulance. Fast!

I check my pocket. I haven't got my mobile with me. Left it on the table in the office.

Stupid, stupid girl!

I reach for his right arm and search for the pulse. For a few seconds I get nothing. The skin feels clammy and cold, like it is wax and not a real person at all.

Then I have it. There *is* still a faint pulse! If I can cut him down he might still survive.

There's no time for an ambulance. No time. I think about the farmer who lives next door. One of his fields is just on the other side of the copse.

'Help!' I scream. 'I need help! Please! **Help!**'

14 JOE

The two cops stare at Shammy. He looks sad and shivery and lost. I take a deep breath of air, make a big effort to get my wits back.

'So what's the story? What's with the blue face?'

'Fancy-dress party,' I tell them.

'Oh yeah? What d'you go as then?'

And something in my brain's still working because I come back with:

'A smurf.'

The younger cop snorts a laugh then turns it into a cough.

'I hope you're not taking the mickey,' the older one says.

'No sir. I've got too much respect for the boys in blue, sir.'

I don't know if there's something about the way I say it but now both the cops crack a smile.

'Bit of a joker aren't you, son? What's your name? How old are you?'

'Joe Fontana. I'm sixteen.'

'Address?'

I mumble it. The boy wonder enters it into a little handheld computer thing and starts to check me out.

'What's happened to you? You look like you've taken a bit of a beating.'

'Fell off a beer crate,' I tell him.

15 BECCA

My cry for help gets no reply.

I pick up the penknife.

I have to sort this out myself. And that's the most frightening thought of my life.

I scramble for the chair, set it upright on the forest floor. I step up. Start to cut. The sickly sweet smell of blood assaults me.

The rope is nylon, thick and strong. The first few sawing motions have no effect at all and a wave of despair overwhelms me as I hack away at the stubborn strands.

His blood soaks into the fabric of my T-shirt.

This isn't going to work. He's going to die.

I press the metal blade deeper, summoning all my strength and willing the blade to cut and cut and cut. Then it's working. The first of the strands frays, then splits. Yes!

I cut. Saw. Hack. Dad still swings and I know that even now he is slipping away.

He has to live. Please God let him live!

The final strand breaks.

Dad falls to the ground. The impact is heavy, his head smashing with a sickening thud against an exposed root of the old oak.

16 JOE

'Mind if I take a look at your bag?' The cop slips the bag off my shoulder, pulls out a couple of cans.

'Regular little Picasso we got here.' He admires the wall. 'This your work?'

I nod. No point in denying it now. Then the boy wonder shows his mate the screen of the little tablet.

'This isn't your first time is it? I got plenty of info on you here Mr Cheeky Chops Fontana. Seems like you've been busy spraying half the walls in London.'

I love that. Almost makes me feel better. The way he calls me *Mr Cheeky Chops Fontana* ...

'Look. You've gone too far this time, sonny. I'm going to issue you with a caution. Do you understand what that means?'

My hands curl into a fist. I know what it means. This isn't my first time. It means implications. It means the youth offending team. Dad getting questions too.

Dad. I get this icy dread when I think how he might react. He gets stressed, my dad. Dangerously stressed. Potential heart attack stressed. He's got these special pills for it and everything.

'Get in the car,' the cop goes. 'We'll take you home.'

'What about my dog?'

Shammy's staring at them with those melty brown eyes.

'Go on,' says the main guy. 'But he stays on your lap.'

I jump down and grab hold of the rope. It's still gripped tightly around Dad's neck and I can hardly get my fingers behind it. A huge egg-shaped bump is growing just above his right ear.

Come on! Come on!

It's too tight. I can't loosen the knot. My vision is getting blurry with the tears.

Yes! I slide the knot away. Rip the noose over his head.

What next? What next?

I have to be logical, make the right decisions but my heart is racing so fast that my brain is doing pirouettes.

Is he breathing? Has he still got a pulse?

Then I remember a trick from an old detective movie. I pick up his glasses and hold the unbroken lens close to his mouth.

The lens quickly gathers a thin sheen of condensation.

He's breathing! This insane desire to scream for joy almost takes over. But it is not the time. He could still die at any minute.

I run back to the house and find my mobile.

'Emergency services. Which service do you require?'

18 JOE

The cops drive me and Shammy home. They ask more about my family and I tell them about Dad being Italian and Mum English. About growing up here in London and spending holidays with cousins over there.

We pass the booze shop and the old empty church where the crack dealers hang out. Then we're in the estate and it's a relief to see that things are quiet.

It's not good to be noticed round here. If a local gang saw me in a police car, questions would be asked.

The lights are on at home. The house Dad bought off the council. It's a bit shabby but better than a high-rise. The door swings open and it's Princess Pea, wearing those fleecy pink PJs that she lives in twenty-four-seven.

Princess Pea. That's the name my dad gave his girlfriend. Her real name is Pauline.

'Evening madam. Can we come in and have a word?'

'What's he done now?' She looks like thunder. 'And what's happened to his face?'

She leads the police into the front room. They let me take Shammy up to the bathroom and blast him with the shower for a bit. Then I give him a tin of food and he goes to his blanket. I think he'll be all right.

Then I hear the front door go. It's my dad home and I know that things can go one way or the other now.

And if it goes bad, it's going to go *really* bad.

19 BECCA

An ambulance is on the way. I run down the drive and take up position at the gate. I need to be here or they'll speed right past. No one can ever find our house in this maze of lanes.

With every passing second I am playing emotional catch-up. *My father attempting suicide?*

Do I believe it? No! No! No and **No!** Even in the darkest times after Mum left I don't believe he ever thought of it.

I *cannot* believe it. Because to believe it is to open a door into an unimaginably dark place. A place where all of the things I cherish ... his love for me ... his joy in watching me learn ... *all* those things ...

They were all false. An illusion. He must have been pretending.

Because *if* he did choose to try and end his own life, then he can't have loved me at all.

But what is the alternative? That the events of this week have caused someone to hate or fear Dad so much that they would try to kill him?

It's true there is a motive. Just four days ago Dad told the truth about the dubious death of one of his former colleagues. Became a whistle-blower exposing a government cover-up.

As I hear the ambulance siren racing towards the house I remember what Dad said about the shady agencies he worked for. And the sinister nature of his words creates a cloud of suspicion in my head.

'You can't trust these people, Rebecca. Given half a chance they just lie, kill and walk away.'

20 JOE

Dad storms in.

The sight of the two cops gives him the glittery Italian eyes. He shaved his hair off a while back because he was going bald and now his whole head's gone sweaty. He looks totally wired and he starts pacing up and down. He's a big man – very big. The floor is shaking under his weight.

'What's going on?' he shouts. 'You're blue, Joe. You're sodding blue!'

''S'nothing,' I say. 'I just got beaten up.'

'We found him spraying graffiti,' says the cop. 'We've given him a caution.'

'Caution?' goes Dad. And he's winding up good and proper now. 'I don't care about any bloody caution. Don't you think it's more important to find out who's had a go at my son?'

I get a happy buzz. Dad's on my side. It feels good.

Pauline gives him a glass of water and he pops one of his heart pills. He wipes at his forehead with his shirt sleeve.

We fill in a load of forms. Finally the cops go. Dad takes me to the bathroom and scrubs some of the blue off my face.

'Get some sleep,' he says. 'I'll let you lie in late tomorrow.'

I go to my bedroom. And Shammy's there on his blanket and he's so exhausted he doesn't even wake up.

21 BECCA

The paramedics put Dad in the recovery position. They have checked his airway and covered him with a heat-conserving blanket.

But the forest floor is still dotted with spatters of thick blood. It sickens me to see it.

'His pulse is weak,' one of the paramedics tells me. 'But he's still with us. The main problems now are blood loss and this injury to the head.'

He gestures to the bump. The bruised, bluey-grey flesh; the injury that I caused through my own stupidity.

In the distance I can hear a helicopter. It is coming closer.

The paramedics place Dad on a stretcher, hoist it waist high and we start the journey back up to the ambulance. As we exit the trees on to the lawn we find the driver running towards us.

'I've got control on the line,' he says. 'Turns out this is a code eight.'

The two paramedics look at each other.

'You sure?' one of them asks. 'Code *eight?*'

At that moment a dark green helicopter swoops low over the copse.

22 JOE

'There's a nice flask of tea in the glovebox,' Dad says.

It's a couple of days later. We're down at the courthouse where the youth offending team are waiting to have a little chat.

Dad has come out of work early to pick me up in his Transit and we've parked with fifteen minutes to spare.

He pours me a plastic cup full of sweet tea then sits silently for a bit. Eventually he says,

'I've been thinking, Joe. It's got to stop – the graffiti I mean. Sooner or later you'll get a criminal record and then you'll be stuffed. No one will employ you.'

I gulp down the tea even though it's still too hot.

I look closely at Dad. There's a few drops of sweat on his neck and his face is grey.

'When we get home I want you to go to the bins and dump all your spray cans.'

'*What?*' I feel like he's told me to cut off my leg.

I take a deep breath. I know it will make him happier, maybe even help with his sickness. But ... no more tagging?

'I'll think about it,' I tell him.

23 BECCA

The helicopter banks into a hover over the croquet lawn, blasting a hurricane of leaves and cut grass into the air.

'What's going on?' I ask the paramedics. But they can't hear me above the noise.

The aircraft touches down with a small bounce of the wheels. The engine whine starts to diminish. Within seconds the rear door is opened and three men climb out on to the lawn.

Two are dressed in military uniform. The third is a man in civilian clothes. I recognise him from a visit to see Dad just a few days ago. He is Marcus Benson, Dad's boss at the Bio-weapons Research Laboratory. He is as greasy as a plate of fried egg and chips.

I move towards him but Benson blanks me totally and sweeps past. He barks a command to the two soldiers.

'Put him through the decon. Fast as you can. We need to think about containment here.'

'Containment?' I run to catch up with him.

'Exposure to biological or chemical weapons,' Benson snaps, as if it's perfectly obvious. 'Radioactive substances and so on.'

Radioactive substances?

What does he mean by that?

Even as he speaks, this huge army-green truck marked INCIDENT CONTROL is turning into the property and parking up in the drive.

'Move!' Benson yells at his men.

24 JOE

We enter the court and are taken in front of the youth offending team.

'Good morning, Joe.' The woman in charge knows me quite well. She flashes me the steely eye when she sees the patches of blue I haven't been able to scrub off my face.

I reckon it's only a matter of time before she's slapping an ASBO on me or maybe even an ankle tag.

The Crown Prosecution report and my statement have already been through the system. I told the truth; there was no sense in trying to hide what I did.

A stab of real fear hits me. What if they send me to Feltham Young Offenders Institution? Away from Dad?

Then the sentence:

'One hundred hours of community service will give you time to think about the damage you have caused. I will instruct the community liaison officer to have you clean your own mess up. Perhaps then you will think twice before spoiling the public domain.'

'Actually, the Home Office has recently changed the title of community service to "Youth Rehabilitation Order with an unpaid work requirement",' says the man on her right.

'I'm aware of that,' snaps the boss. 'Goodbye Mr Fontana, goodbye Joe. Thank you so much for coming in.'

One hundred hours. Nightmare.

25 BECCA

Four men dressed in white protection suits and gas masks lift my Dad up and take him towards the green truck. The garden is now buzzing with activity.

'He needs to be in hospital,' I tell Benson. 'Every minute you waste here puts his life in danger.'

'He will get the care he needs, as soon as we've run the decon. You're going in as well by the way.'

What? Me too? I have to be decontaminated as well? This nightmare is getting worse with each passing second.

'Come with me,' a woman in a gas mask orders. 'There's no time to lose.'

She takes me firmly by the arm, pulls me towards the truck.

We climb the short set of stairs and enter the back of the vehicle. We are in a small cubicle decked in white tiles, about the size of a family changing room at a swimming pool.

'This is the strip-down room,' she says, her voice muffled behind the mask. 'Take off every item of clothing and place them in this black plastic bag.'

I stare right at her. 'And if I refuse?'

'Your life may be at stake!' she snaps.

I pause for a few seconds, then slowly do as she asks, numb with the shock of what is happening to me.

'Your clothes will be immediately incinerated,' she says. 'Come this way.'

I am naked and trembling as the woman leads me through a plastic doorway into the second chamber of the truck.

26 JOE

10 a.m. Monday. I report to a council centre with four other youth offenders and we are given a little speech by this weasel-faced old bloke called Derek. Then he hands out rubber gloves, cleaning fluids and scrubbing brushes.

We drive across town for a while, then arrive at the wall. My wall. My Gary Barker tag still shiny and bright ... and unfinished.

'Military hospital, this place,' Derek says. 'You'd better do a good job or they'll set the squaddies on you.'

Derek drops me off with some idiot called Carl.

'Put some welly into it!' he says. 'I'll be back in an hour.'

Thirty seconds after Derek's vanished, Carl lights up a ciga-rette and starts to walk off towards the park.

'Where you going?' I call after him.

'Dunno,' he shrugs. He kicks a pebble across the road and disappears in the direction of the nearest shops.

I'd like to go and buy some chips, but the threat of Derek coming back is enough to stop me. I don't want my sentence doubled.

Scrub. Scrub. Scrub. Ten minutes of muscle power and my arm's already feeling dead. And the worst thing is I know there's special chemicals that could make it a faster job if they'd only give them to us. But they want us to suffer, so it's down to elbow grease.

Ninety-nine hours and fifty minutes to go ... oh man. This is going to *kill* me.

27 BECCA

'This cubicle is the washdown room,' the woman tells me. 'You have to shower here and use this antibacterial soap on your body and hair.'

I stand underneath the shower unit and the cold water rushes out with uncomfortable force. Then comes the drying room. Incredible heat, blasting from a huge fan.

I can hear the sound of the helicopter engine starting up.

I have to be fast. I don't want them to take Dad away without me.

'This is a Tyvek protection suit,' the woman explains. 'Put it on and ensure that you use the Velcro fastenings on the wrists and neck.'

I slip on the suit and rush out of the decon unit to catch Benson up.

'I want to go with him,' I insist.

'Sorry,' he says. 'No can do.'

'I *have* to go with him. **Please**!'

I take a step towards the helicopter. Dad's already inside. Benson nods to two of the men in white protection suits and they gently but firmly take me by the arms. 'I'm afraid that won't be possible,' he says. I push against them. But they are too strong.

'They're going to take you for some more tests,' Benson says. 'Good luck.'

He jumps into the back of the helicopter with two of the soldiers. Then it lifts off the ground in a rush of roasted air.

28 JOE

I'm scrubbing away. Half an hour goes by.

Then I hear this noise. A helicopter! Flying in really low over the building. It's landing in the park.

Then the gate opens at the hospital entrance. A green ambulance and a couple of jeeps drive out with real soldiers in them. It's well exciting! As soon as the helicopter touches down they take out this trolley with a man on it. There's a huge bandage on his head.

Four soldiers lift up the trolley and carry it to the ambulance. Then they shove it in the back and it races back towards the hospital as the helicopter takes off.

I wait till the street goes quiet. Then I climb up the stepladder and sneak a look over the wall. I can see into this yard where the ambulance is pulling in.

I'm in a perfect spying place; in the corner where it's darker than the rest and there's this metal pole mostly hiding my face.

They bring out the patient. He looks nearly dead.

Then I hear a motor coming along the road. It could be Derek on his way back. I duck back down the stepladder and start to scrub at the graffiti.

The show's over. For the moment. But I find myself thinking about the man they brought in by helicopter ...

Who was he? What happened to him?

I'm dying to find out more.

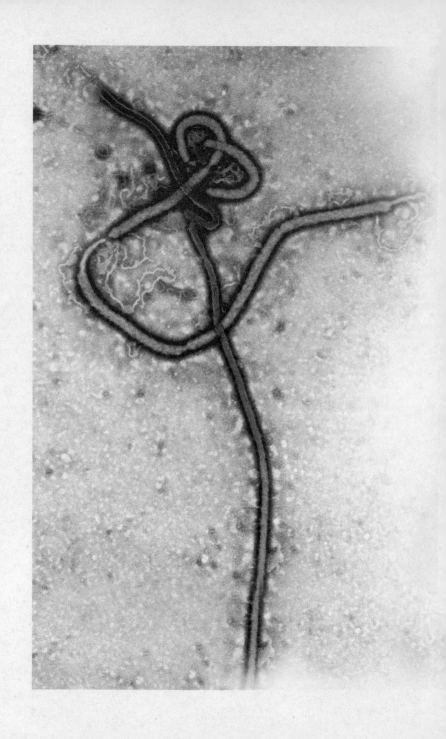

PART 2

BARRIER ONE

Patrick Eden: I'm walking down the first corridor. There's a level-4 biohazard door in front of me.

Police Command: What are we dealing with?

Patrick Eden: We're talking about a highly sophisticated lab. Capable of handling the most lethal pathogens on the planet. I'm opening the metal door now and stepping into the sterilisation chamber.

Audio transcript from helmet mic worn by Patrick Eden, UK Government bioweapons inspector following emergency call at SYMBARON lab, Hampshire.

'Rebecca,' Benson says. 'How are you feeling, my dear?'

It's 10.30 a.m. the following morning.

I'm not in the mood for his smarmy words. Why? Because for the last twenty-four hours I have been held at some government facility in Wiltshire, subjected to a barrage of tests. They've taken blood, samples of saliva and urine, analysed strands of hair.

I've been Geiger-countered for beta particles. Checked for gamma radiation. Pricked and pushed from one medical specialist to another.

Apparently I am in the clear. No evidence of chemical, biological or nuclear contamination at all.

Now I've been handed some ridiculous schoolgirl clothes that hardly fit me and taken to a meeting with Benson. And I'm furious.

'Where's my dad? I want to see him. *Now* please. And I want to get a message to my mum. She needs to know about this.'

'You will be taken to see your father as soon as possible, Rebecca. As for your mother, well, contact her yourself ... if you can.'

There is an awkward pause as I wonder how much Benson knows? Does he know Mum was a scientist just like Dad? Does he know about her mental illness? That she's locked herself away from the world for the last five years, living on a narrowboat, moving from place to place? That I have not seen her in all that time?

And what does he want with *me*?

30 JOE

It's morning. Dad comes in with a cup of tea. 'How you doing, Joe?' he asks.

I groan. My arms are murder from all the scrubbing yesterday.

'Pauline's making you some brekky,' Dad says. The smell of frying bacon wafts up the stairs. She's doing that thing that makes me feel strange – pretending to be a mum. Pretending to be *my* mum.

'I'm not that hungry,' I tell him. 'I'll get something at Subway later.'

Dad sighs and looks out of the window for a bit. Then he sits on the edge of the bed. He looks well tired and his eyes are red.

'Look Joe,' he starts slowly, 'I know you're struggling with me having someone else, but can't you just give her a chance?'

I look at my special photo – me and Mum on the beach in Norfolk. Before the cancer finally killed her. I'm holding a spade with a massive jellyfish on it.

'I remember that stupid jellyfish,' Dad chuckles as he picks up the photo. 'Ended up in my shoe, yeah?'

I can't help smiling.

'I need someone in my life, Joe,' he says. 'Pauline's good for me.'

I think about it in the shower. And I know that Dad's right about it all; I *have* been getting addicted to the graffiti. And I have been giving Pauline a hard time.

Maybe it's time for things to change.

31 BECCA

'How is he?' I ask Benson.

'Your father's alive, thank goodness, but he's not out of danger yet. He's in a coma.'

A single horrifying image flashes through my mind. Dad's head smashing against that tree root when I cut him down. He's in a coma and it's all my fault.

The guilt causes my stomach to cramp. I breathe deeply to try and control it.

'Who tried to kill him?' I continue. 'Have you found anything out yet?'

'No one tried to kill him, Rebecca. Our people are looking at it. And they can't find any evidence that this was anything other than it seems.'

'That he tried to commit suicide? I don't believe it.'

'Well I'm afraid the evidence says otherwise. He was a man with significant problems. Look at the stress he brought on himself in this past week.'

'He was a man with a *daughter*. He would never have done that to me.'

'He did it, Rebecca. You have to come to terms with that.'

Benson leans forward. The atmosphere in the room chills yet further as he wets his lips. I get the sense that the conversation is about to take a heavy turn.

'Rebecca, did your father ever talk to you about the death of Simon Hazelgrove?'

Ah. Here we go.

Down to breakfast. Fry-up with Dad even though he's supposed to be eating healthy for his heart. Princess Pea makes a fuss of Shammy and gives him the fat off the bacon and I think well, maybe she's not *so* bad.

Then I see a photo on the front page of Dad's newspaper. It's the hospital. The military place. And my graffiti is in the corner of the picture!

Dad's well impressed by my new fame. He reads the article out loud:

GOVERNMENT BOFFIN IN MYSTERY SUICIDE ATTEMPT

A scientist with links to secret bioweapons programmes is in a coma at a military hospital in north London today following a mystery suicide bid at his Surrey home. Patrick Eden (43) was found hanging by his daughter Rebecca (15) at approximately 9 a.m. yesterday morning.

It's him! The man they flew in by helicopter!

Mr Eden's profile as a whistle-blower is likely to focus attention on the case. A virologist by training, he embarrassed the government earlier this week by challenging official claims that weapons scientist Simon Hazelgrove was killed by an accidental release of gas at a private laboratory in Hampshire.

I check my watch. It's time to report to work.

I wonder if that scientist bloke will still be alive ... I'll be up that ladder and sneaking a look as soon as I can.

33 BECCA

'Dad didn't talk to me about Simon Hazelgrove,' I tell Benson.

He goes quiet, just sits there staring at me so it gets uncomfortable and I feel like I have to fill the gap.

'I mean I know he was on the inspection team that got called in to the lab where that scientist died. But apart from that I only know what he said to the press on Monday.'

'Ah, yes. The day your father became a whistle-blower. An unfortunate term don't you think? It makes it sound as if there was a scandal to be revealed, whereas in reality the government has done nothing wrong.'

'My father told the truth,' I protest. 'I'm totally sure of that.'

Benson's eyes narrow.

'Your father is a brilliant man, Rebecca, but a naive one. Blabbing to journalists has caused us no end of trouble and left the prime minister with a lot of egg on his face.'

Benson shifts some papers about on his desk. And now I can tell by the way he is staring at me that the *real* subject is about to begin.

'Did your father mention a sample?' Benson asks. 'A sample he may have removed illegally from our laboratory?'

I feel this cold sensation sweep through my whole body.

Now I have to be *really* careful what I say.

34 JOE

I report to the centre at 8.30 a.m. The other offenders turn up nearer nine and get a blasting from that cranky old bloke Derek for being late. He drives us out in the van and drops off the rest along the way.

'That prat Carl's in it for bunking off yesterday,' he tells me. 'They're going to send him up to Feltham. There's some real scum in that place, lad. You don't want to be slammed up there, I can tell you.'

He's right. I've heard all about Feltham Young Offenders Institution, and I definitely don't want any bit of it.

All the more reason to do my hundred hours and get out with a clean sheet.

We arrive at the hospital. There's a couple of photographers hanging around the entrance, huge great cameras slung round their necks.

Must be waiting to get pics of the scientist. It's exciting to think the news people are here.

Derek helps me with the ladder and chemicals. Then he takes a look at the wall and rolls himself a cigarette.

'You're winning, lad. That G's looking a bit faded now. And the A's on the way out as well.'

He glances at his watch.

'Better go check on the others.'

I just wish he'd get a move on. So I can take another peek over the top of the wall.

35 BECCA

'Your father ordered certain items of laboratory equipment in the last few days,' Benson continues. 'Equipment that might be used in the analysis of dangerous pathogens. Do you have any idea what he was up to, Rebecca?'

'No idea.' My reply is deadpan but inside my mind is racing.

'We should have monitored your father more closely,' Benson continues with a frown. 'There are some rather ugly rumours going around the bioweapons community.'

Benson stares at me long and hard. I hold his gaze, anger welling up.

'Do the words "Dark Heart" mean anything to you, Rebecca?'

I bite the inside of my lip.

'No.'

'Tell us what you know,' he insists. 'Your help could save lives.'

'I want to see him,' I say. I've had enough of this interrogation.

'All right,' he says reluctantly. 'We'll continue this chat another time.'

Benson picks up a telephone and punches in a number. 'I have arranged a car and a driver for you. You might need protection from the press.'

He barks into the phone: 'Send Sergeant Griffin in, will you?'

And I'm thinking, *'Protection from the press?'*

36 JOE

Soon as Derek's gone I take the ladder to the corner and get right back up the wall to sneak a look.

I just can't resist it – 'specially now I know the patient is some sort of famous weapons genius.

I can see a few soldiers in the yard. They're smoking a crafty fag behind some pillars where I guess their bosses can't see them. Then I shift position a bit and make a discovery: I can see right into the scientist's room!

He's there in the bed. So he's still alive then ... not that he's moving or talking or anything.

I watch for a while. But all that happens is this doctor changes the drip. So I step back down the ladder. And I just keep scrubbing.

A short while later this motorbike cruises slowly along the road. It's a BMW RS1200, one of my favourite bikes. That's why I notice it.

The rider is a really big guy, dressed in black leathers. He rides along the road. Then turns around and makes another even slower pass, looking at me all the time. He's wearing mirrored shades so I can't see his eyes. It's almost like he's checking me out. In the end it gets on my nerves.

'Got a problem mate?' I shout. He revs the bike and drives away.

37 BECCA

Sergeant Griffin enters the room.

'I'm sorry to hear about your dad,' she says. Her accent is Scottish. 'Call me Liz.'

We shake hands and I sense real power in her grip. She's a sporty, attractive-looking woman, dressed in a smart navy-blue trouser suit with her blonde hair pulled back into a tight ponytail.

'Miss Griffin will take you to see your father,' Benson says.

Liz leads me out of the hospital to the car park and across to a vehicle which is so highly polished I can see my reflection mirrored perfectly in the paint.

'You sit in the back,' she says. As she opens the door for me, her unbuttoned jacket flaps open just enough that I can see a brown leather holster slung beneath her shoulder.

She's carrying a gun! My minder is carrying a gun. *Why?*

We hit the road. And I'm thinking about my dad, and Mum as well ... how everything was perfect until the horse-riding accident six years ago and the head injury she suffered as a result. She became a different person, changing from a warm and loving mother to a cold and uncaring stranger. When I tried to cuddle her she just pushed me away.

She saw a psychiatrist; personality change disorder was diagnosed. But by then it was too late; she withdrew from the world and left us, choosing to live a solitary life as a recluse. It broke Dad's heart. And mine as well.

Will she have seen the press about what's happened to Dad? I have no idea. But I have to get a message to her. If I can.

38 JOE

I'm done on the G. It's faded almost to nothing.

Then, as I turn to dip my brush, something catches my eye – up high – on the other side of the road.

A flash of light. A reflection from a window in a building next to the park. I say window. It's a hole really, since the building's still being done.

There's loads of office blocks like that round here; half built and waiting for more money so they can be finished.

Anyway this reflection gets my attention. And I wouldn't have thought anything about it, except then I see a shadow; a figure dressed in black, in the same window space, holding a pair of binoculars in his hands. And he jumps back into the darkness like he's scared of being seen, but not before I get a glimpse of his mirrored shades.

I could swear it's that big guy off the motorbike.

Why would someone be hanging around on the sixth floor of an empty office block, unless they wanted a perfect view down into the military hospital?

Because it really would be a perfect view.

I check out the security fence that surrounds the office building. It's covered in stickers saying NO TRESPASSING. No sign of a place to get in. But obviously that biker found a way.

What's he up to?

34 BECCA

It's not going to be easy to find Mum. Last thing we heard she was moored up somewhere on the Thames, moving from one place to another – a nomadic life which obviously suits her new restless spirit.

Never a call. Not a single letter or birthday card. Just an awful void.

Once, missing her terribly, I cycled down to the nearest canal and sat on the bridge watching the narrowboats pass by. I was hoping against hope that I would see her. But I never did.

She probably wouldn't even recognise me now.

Then I have a thought: maybe now is the time to try and track her down online. Dad had spotted her name as a reviewer on some scientific papers recently, so she's obviously working from time to time. I figure I might be able to locate her through those academic publications.

If they are employing her for her reviews then she must have some sort of mailing address.

There's an iPad on the passenger seat.

'Miss Griffin, can I borrow your tablet please?'

'I'll have to check with base,' she replies.

She puts in a call, chatting on a headset as we crawl through the western suburbs of London. Finally she ends the conversation and tells me: 'Sorry. It's a departmental device, I can't let you use it.'

'Oh. Then can I get my mobile back?'

'I'll have to check that with base as well.'

I am beginning to get it. 'Base' is taking over my life.

I scrub away all morning then the minibus cruises back round the corner.

Derek's got some of the other young offenders on board and we sit in the van and eat cheese rolls and soup. The rolls are like rocks and the soup's got lumps of tomato-flavoured paste where it hasn't been stirred. Derek doesn't eat because he can't stop talking. All he goes on about is how he's thinking about inventing some sort of machine for getting graffiti off walls.

'Make myself a fortune,' he goes. 'Then I can stop driving idiots like you lot around. No offence, like.'

At half past one Derek takes the lads back to their jobs. All goes quiet.

I'm just about to get back to the scrubbing. Then what happens is I hear a car pulling up. And I get a little shot of nerves because it could be Gary Barker. But it's not. Not in a shiny top-of-the-range Lexus like this one.

Then this woman driver gets out and opens the back door … and this girl steps out.

This girl steps out.

And just for a tiny part of a second her eyes are on mine. And they are very blue. And she looks lost and upset and far away and totally disconnected from everything in the world and for some stupid reason I just get this … what, feeling? I don't know.

But I know I haven't felt it before.

41 BECCA

We arrive at the hospital, and the first thing I see is this boy cleaning the wall – scrubbing off some graffiti.

The boy looks at me for a second or two. I notice that his eyes are an unusually dark shade of brown, almost black. He definitely has a bit of an exotic look: jet-black hair, that golden depth to his skin, so I'm guessing maybe his family have Mediterranean roots.

He's wearing one of those pairs of jeans that hang down a bit. And his trainers are full of holes. And he's got splashes of cleaning chemical on his T-shirt.

He's a mess. And he looks rather *bad*. And it crosses my mind that he might scratch Liz's car with a key or something while we're in the hospital.

But. *But* ... when we look at each other. Well, and it's the most *unexpected* thing. Because despite all the drama of the last thirty hours or so, despite the sheer misery of my dad's 'suicide attempt', and the coma and the anger, cutting through all of that there's this tiny little moment of ... I haven't got a name for it.

It's just a tremor. Deeply buried in the mantle of the earth. A seismic shock occurring so far away it can hardly be felt.

I decide not to think about it.

42 JOE

'Wash your car for a fiver, madam?' I have to say something or I'm just standing there staring at this girl.

And the lady driver smiles and says, 'Piss off.'

And I reply pleasantly, 'I'll take that as a "no" shall I, madam?'

The driver gives me a crappy look. But it's given me a couple more seconds to check out the girl.

Her clothes are weird. Like from a film where you see old school uniforms. Just a white shirt and one of those green sort of kilt-type things that look Scottish.

What does she look like?

But it's a short circuit. Because she looks terrible and amazing at the same time. And half of me is thinking, 'That girl is wearing old-fashioned clothes that most girls wouldn't be seen dead in.' And the other bit of me is thinking, 'But check out her face. Now that is a beautiful face and I'm not being rude here but she really has got curves where boys like to see curves. And ... and that wavy brown hair ... or is it red? Anyway she's got a lot of it.

And she is *hot*. And *sad*, all at the same time. And I *never* saw a girl like that.

43 BECCA

Liz leads me towards the entrance and my heart sinks when I see how many photographers are waiting there. They blast off hundreds of shots as we walk towards them, shouting all the while.

'Look this way, Rebecca! Just one picture! Over here!'

'Ignore them,' Liz says. But it's not so easy, it's intrusive and weird to have all those lenses turned my way.

We sign in and a stern-looking nurse leads us briskly across an interior courtyard. A bunch of bored soldiers stare at us as we walk by. Well they stare at me, to be more accurate. One of them mutters something lewd. I feel my cheeks reddening.

'Pack it in, lads,' Liz tells them, a crackle of real authority in her voice.

We enter a corridor, painted that eerie shade of hospital green. Nurses stride past in Crocs, the resin soles squishing as they pad the tiles.

'This is your father's room,' the nurse tells me.

She pushes open the door. And I have braced myself for this moment but it is still a shock. To see my dad lying there, invaded by tubes, his head bandaged. So vulnerable.

I go to his side. Still half expecting him to wake up and flash that wide smile of his. But he is utterly still. As still as an Egyptian mummy lying in some forgotten tomb.

I get a terrible flashback to Mum after her riding accident. Lying in a similar hospital bed. It's almost too much to bear.

44 JOE

So I'm up on top of the wall, spying and loving it. Just can't help myself.

My head's tucked nicely away behind the metal strut so no one inside the hospital can see me.

In the courtyard the soldiers are washing the vans. Then I check out the room and ... the girl walks in! She's visiting the patient. Gets shown to a chair by one of the nurses.

Then I remember the newspaper article – about the daughter who saved the scientist from hanging.

That's why all the press were taking the shots of her: she's a hero. She saved her dad. Got to respect her for that.

I try to imagine how it would be if it was *my* dad lying there sick and I get a twist in my gut just to think of it. I duck down just a fraction more. Get more cover. Must not be seen.

I don't want to miss a second.

The man – her father – doesn't move.

A coma. It's like being dead but you're not dead. Sometimes they can even hear what you're saying about them but they can't show it. Just move an eye, or their tongue or whatever. I can't even think how terrible it has to be.

And I keep watching because there's something about all of this that's got me gripped.

45 BECCA

There is a monitor attached to Dad's wrist. A drip is being administered via an intravenous needle. An oxygen tube is taped into his nostrils.

I want to rip all those horrible things away and give him a big hug, but instead I wrap my hand around his.

'I'll be waiting outside,' Liz says tactfully. She leaves the room.

I sit, registering the details as I try to remain composed in front of the nurse.

She is sitting in the corner, reading a copy of *Heat*. She looks ridiculously young. Hopeless to wish it, but I would love her to leave for a while. It's so hard to be natural with a stranger around.

I glance out of the window, catch a glimpse of movement in a remote corner. It's that boy – the one scrubbing the graffiti. He's spying over the wall. What an idiot.

I frown at him. His eyes widen.

The door suddenly opens. A doctor with long blond hair pops his head round.

'Hello Rebecca. I'm Doctor Sadler. I'm the consultant neurologist here. Can we have a word?'

46 JOE

The girl has spotted me! I get a mixed-up thrill of fear and excitement all at the same time. Then this doctor with blond hair comes in. The girl gets up and starts to talk to him.

Time to get back to work. I slide back down the stepladder and dip my brush in the bucket of cleaning fluid. But I can't stop thinking about her and that's unusual for me.

A lot of the lads I know are always going on about girls – which ones are hot. A lot of those lads are well into porn. Always swapping clips on their mobiles and stuff. Some of them have even done it with a girl. Or so they say …

That's not my thing. I nearly never think about girls. I don't know why. I've just got other stuff on my mind. Only right now I haven't. Because right now there's *nothing* else on my mind.

At that moment a familiar wagon comes round the corner; it's Dad, come to see how I'm getting on.

'All right Joe? I got the flowers you wanted.'

He shows me the bunch and I tell him thanks. Mum loved lilies. I try to put them fresh every week.

'In there,' I tell him. He places them in the water bucket. Then he stares up at the graffiti, tutting beneath his breath. 'Reckon you need a hand,' he says with a smile.

Too right I do.

47 BECCA

'Rebecca. I guess you don't mind if I call you by your first name? We've run some tests on your father, a CT scan and so on, and I need to discuss the results with you.'

'OK.'

'Come over to the lightbox and I'll show you what we've found.'

I join the consultant by the viewing screen in the corner of the room. He pulls a series of large scans from a massive white envelope. He slips the first of them on to the lightbox and I see the distinctive outline of a human skull.

'This is the area of the scan we're worried about.'

He points to a lighter area on the film. I see a mass about the size of a lemon in the top of Dad's skull.

'He's suffered serious trauma, neurological damage in this area of the brain. It's a haemorrhage I'm afraid, and the bleeding has caused him to go into a coma.'

There is not a shred of emotion in his voice. He could be talking about a faulty exhaust on a car.

'His head hit a tree root, when I cut him down,' I tell him.

'Yes, so I understand. Most unfortunate.'

'How long will he be in the coma for?'

48 JOE

Dad helps me with the graffiti for a bit. Then he says, 'I've got an idea. What do you say we make a trip to Norwich after we've been to the graveyard?'

I tell him yes. I like our trips up to Norwich. It's exciting because Dad's dodgy mate Bruno lets me drive his cars.

Dodgy Bruno. That's who my dad works for. Well, he's forced to work for him in fact. But I'm not exactly sure why.

So far as I know it's tied up with something that happened in Italy three years ago. Dad had wanted to make a new start there and we moved to Milan even though Mum was iffy about it. After just six months we had to make a lightning getaway back to London. Fast enough that I couldn't even say goodbye to all my new Italian friends at school.

Dad was in trouble. I've worked that out. And now he's having to pay back some sort of debt, selling illegal red diesel to punters. Even though he could go to jail for it.

Red diesel is ultra cheap, tax-free and for farm vehicles only. It's got some special red dye in it so Customs and Excise can spot it.

So once a week Dad goes to Norwich with his special van and fills up this great big tank in the back. Then he sells it in London at a bargain price. Makes a fortune for Bruno. Pays a pittance for my dad.

It gets Dad well stressed but he says he's only got another few months to go. Then the debt will be paid.

49 BECCA

'There's no way of telling with a coma,' the consultant tells me. 'It could be a matter of weeks. It could even be years. There is a case of a patient coming out of a coma after thirty-seven years.'

Thirty-seven years.

What if that person had been secretly conscious for all that time? Able to hear and comprehend the world around them but unable to show it?

'Even if he came round there would be no guarantee that he could resume a normal life,' the consultant goes on. 'All we can do is keep him alive and wait and see.'

I turn back to Dad. And the guilt is almost unbearable; I can still hear the dull thud as his head hit the root. I should have realised the danger when I cut him down. But I was desperate to let him breathe.

I twist the corner of his blanket in my hands. I did so many things right, but I did the crucial thing wrong.

They give me thirty more minutes with Dad. I am searching for any sign of response; a flicker of the eye, a twitch of the mouth. But all I see is the shallow rise and fall of his chest as he breathes.

Then Liz is at the door. 'Time to go,' she says.

50 JOE

Just as me and Dad are thinking of calling it a day I see the girl and her driver come out of the security gate. And I'm thinking ...

Yes! Another chance to check her out.

But I soon feel bad for staring at her. Because the photographers are crowding in and trying to get shots and she's looking more gutted than ever. Like all of the happiness has been squeezed out of her.

And that tough-looking driver has her arms around the girl and it's weird because on the one hand you could say she's being nice and protective. But you could look at it another way and see the girl as a sort of prisoner.

And there's this strange moment when Dad looks at her and says:

'D'you know what I'm thinking, Joe?'

And I get this flashback – to the day when Mum came out of the hospital. The hollow look in her eyes when she told me and Dad there was no more hope.

'Remembering Mum?'

He puts his hand round my shoulder.

'Yeah.'

Then they're all sweeping past us and one of the snappers trips backwards over my bucket of water and crashes to the floor.

Mum's flowers spill out on to the pavement.

That graffiti boy is staring at me as we push through the chaos.

Then a press guy falls, and I see a bouquet of white lilies is being trodden underfoot. I bend to pick them up and find myself kneeling next to the boy. He's gathering the broken flowers up one by one. I hand him a few stems and a soiled card marked 'MUM' which has fallen into the gutter.

Our fingers touch. Our eyes lock for an electric second or two. I get that strange tight sensation in my chest again.

He mutters 'Thanks,' and, before I can reply, Liz is pulling me up and bundling me into the car.

The last thing I see before we drive away is the boy trying to rearrange the ruined flowers back into some sort of shape. His hands are shaking.

The man with him has his arm around the boy's shoulder.

I let my body ease back into the seat and stare at the traffic. I think about the flowers. For a grave?

When we get close to home Liz hands me a small travelling blanket. 'You're best putting this over your head,' she tells me.

'I'd rather not,' I tell her. 'Why should I hide like some criminal?'

Reporters are gathered in a scrum around the gate, pushing against a line of policemen.

'Rebecca! This way please!' Then, 'Just one picture Rebecca!'

Cameras flash right against the window. I shield my eyes. I'm trembling by the time we break through.

'Not so nice, eh?' Liz says. 'Maybe next time you'll take my advice.'

52 JOE

We buy some more flowers and take them to Mum's grave. Then we make it up to Norwich in a couple of hours and drive to the farm where trampy old Bruno comes out to greet us in his mucky wellies and his greasy cowboy hat.

'All right Joe? How's it going?' Bruno's always glad to see me.

Best of all is he lets me drive his cars around the field while we wait for Dad to fill up his tank. He says I'm a natural and it's true – I could drive from the very first time I did it.

'You in the mood for a bit of a race, Joe?'

Bruno is in a BMW 5 Series. I'm in an Audi TT my dad says was nicked from the front drive of Ipswich Town's goalie.

Three, two, one. We're off. Engines snarling up the cool night air.

The circuit is about half a mile – right through the woods. I'm hitting seventy as we go into muddy turns, burning off Bruno as he overcooks it and runs over some heavy ruts. I know I'm going to total the Audi if I ram a tree but I never get close to losing it. I'm laughing with the buzz of it.

I beat him by about six seconds.

'Gutted!' he goes. 'You should be a getaway driver you're that fast. Speaking of which, do you know how to hot-wire a motor?

'No.'

'Come on then. I'll teach you.'

53 BECCA

We walk to the front of the house. An armed policeman is guarding the front door. 'Good afternoon, miss,' he says.

'Good afternoon.' The answer is a reflex. What I really want to do is scream 'What are you doing here?'

I step into Dad's office and I have to stifle a gasp. Every *single* thing has gone. It has literally been stripped bare. The house feels violated.

I enter the kitchen. Liz is chatting away with the police outside so I have a few moments to snoop about.

Straight away I spot something. The distinctive, purple spine of one of Dad's notebooks. It is nestled in amongst the cookery books and it looks like Benson's people have missed it.

I pull it out and get a warm flush of excitement. It *is* his current book – his work in progress.

I open it up, seeing the usual mix of jotted notes and equations. Then I find a newspaper article folded between two pages. I open it up and see the following headline:

UNEXPLAINED DEATH AT MYSTERY LAB

It's an article about Simon Hazelgrove, Dad's former colleague who died last week. A photo accompanies the piece: the charred remains of the burned-out laboratory on an anonymous industrial estate in Hampshire.

Suddenly I hear Liz's footsteps. I slip the notebook into my bag and head for the stairs.

54 JOE

Bruno leads me across the yard. There's a row of cars lurking in the shadows. 'Choose one,' he says.

I pick a Volvo.

'Perfect. Get in the driver's seat.'

He hands me this massive screwdriver. 'This is the only tool you need,' he goes. 'Now wedge it under that plastic covering the steering column and break it off. Don't worry about the damage, these are all nicked anyway.'

I do as he says. It's surprising how easy it comes off.

'Now pull out the wiring loom next to the key bit.'

I do as he instructs.

'Touch those wires together. Make a short circuit across the ignition contacts.'

'What are you doing?' Dad juts his head in the window.

'Electronics lesson,' Bruno says cheekily, giving me a nudge in the ribs.

'Out!' Dad yanks me by the hood of my jacket. 'Get in the Transit.'

He pushes me roughly towards the van.

'But Dad ... '

'No buts. You stay there and keep your mouth shut.'

One hour later we pull out of Bruno's place and head for the motorway.

'You're never coming back here,' Dad says. 'I'll leave you at home from now on.'

I watch the lights of the farm fade from view.

I close my bedroom door and kick off my shoes. Lying back on my bed, I open the notebook again, wary that Liz could barge in at any moment.

I continue flicking through the pages, and there's one word that jumps out:

Ebola.

Ebola. The presence of the word doesn't surprise me. Of all the bioweapon threats, that was the one that kept Dad awake at night.

'Ebola can be a game changer for our species,' Dad told me once. 'It's the one I fear the most. If it gets weaponised, transferrable through atomised droplets into the lungs, then ninety per cent of humanity could be dead within a week.'

Then I turn another page and an involuntary gasp escapes me. My father has scribbled my mother's name there.

Oh ...

An address is written underneath: Berth 30, Thames Marina, Marlow. And below that is a mobile number.

I stare at the information, my guts twisting unpleasantly as my mind tries to catch up. I don't get it. Dad *knew* where Mum was living? He had her mobile written down and he never *shared* it with me?

The room spins for a few beats. I blink away the dizziness but nausea rises in its place. Dad was in touch with Mum and he never told me.

I wrap the duvet around myself. The room suddenly feels horribly chilled.

56 JOE

It's a new day. Back home. I've had a bit of a doze but not much.

I've been thinking on it, through the night, and I reckon my dad's right; that was stupid mucking around hot-wiring stuff with Bruno. And the tagging's got to stop.

Anyway, I'm going to do it for *him*.

So, as soon as I'm dressed, I gather up the spray cans that are hidden under my bed. There's a few almost empty ones in the kitchen. I grab them too.

I go past the bingo hall and get to the dump. I find the metals container and drop the bag of cans straight into the bin. It makes me feel a bit special knowing what I've done – like everything's new and more real.

And I'm determined to do what Dad said: stay out of trouble.

I take a bus. I still have a bit of time until I have to report to the centre so I get out two stops early, go to McDonald's and get myself a McMuffin and a cup of tea.

While I'm munching on my breakfast I'm remembering last night. Not the hot-wiring, I mean the driving. Then I get this sudden incredible thought.

57 BECCA

Morning. Sleep has been patchy, peppered with unfortunate dreams. I stared at the ceiling half the night, chewing on the reasons why Dad didn't tell me that he was in touch with Mum.

Were there other secrets? What else was he hiding from me?

Liz raps on my door: 'Breakfast! I'll do you a fry-up if you like?'

'Not so hungry,' I tell her. I can't bear the thought of sitting next to my minder at the kitchen table.

I throw on my clothes, put my iPad in my bag and head downstairs to the hall. I can hear the pulse-rush of blood in my ears as I stand next to the telephone. I pick up the handset. I try to dial but my fingers are shaking too much to punch the buttons.

Inhale. Steady and slow. Check the number again. Dial it.

The phone rings for a while then goes to the standard voicemail. I call again and the same thing happens.

'Mum? It's me ... Becca. If you hear this message can you call me back as soon as possible please? It's urgent.' I pause, then can't help adding, 'Mum? Are you OK? I miss you and love you. Bye.'

I enter the kitchen where I find Liz cooking up bacon and eggs.

'Liz, can you drive me somewhere this morning? It's urgent.'

'In principle, yes. I'll just have to ch ... '

' ... check with base?' I finish her sentence for her.

Liz gives me a tight little smile. 'Exactly. Now where do you want to go?'

58 JOE

The incredible thought is this:

What if I was a rally driver?

I mean when I'm older. Or Formula One? Could I do it? Could I hack it? With the pros?

And I think well, maybe I could. At least there has to be some sort of school where you can learn about rally driving.

Now that really is a school I *want* to go to.

And it's a strange moment which makes me want to shiver, because I never *really* wanted to learn anything. But now ... maybe I do. And I'm imagining myself as a top driver, on a podium spraying champagne. Or talking to the people from the telly. Or just doing a lap of honour.

And for the first time in my life I think:

That could be me.

I finish my breakfast but I'm really wired now.

And I suddenly get this urge to speak to Dad. I really want to see what he thinks. Because if he likes the idea then he might help me make it happen; maybe even find me a sponsor.

I run through the streets, heading for Dad's yard.

Liz gets the clearance and we fight through the press pack still waiting at the gate. The flurry of flashbulbs is every bit as disturbing as the night before. Liz drives like a demon to shake off the photographers on motorbikes and we arrive at Marlow after an hour and ten minutes on the road.

Liz's satnav takes us out of town for a mile, then down a tree-lined track. After a few bumps through potholes we arrive at the marina where about fifty boats are moored up.

'Want me to come with you?' Liz asks.

'No thanks,' I tell her. I'm relieved when she agrees she will stay in the car.

The marina gate is wide open so I walk straight in. A few of the cruisers are showing signs of activity: mostly elderly people cleaning and painting, tinkering with engines.

The vessel in berth 30 is a tidy-looking narrowboat, painted green and black. Flower boxes line the roof, bright with carnations and geraniums. A bicycle is chained to the guardrail.

As I step down the floating walkway my heart is screwed up into a dense ball of fear. I'm realising too late that I haven't thought this through at all.

Will Mum recognise me? Will we hug? Will she even want to speak to me? How can we possibly start again after six years apart? It feels like a lifetime.

Somehow my legs stop moving. I call out, my voice trembling: 'Hello?'

All I hear is the chug-chug of a passing boat and the gentle lapping of the river against the walkway.

A brace of ducks flies low overhead, landing noisily on the water in a flurry of wings.

60 JOE

As soon as I get to Dad's yard I tell him straight up that I'm thinking about being a rally driver. And he sips on his tea as he has a think about it.

'It's true you can drive like a nutter,' he says. 'You're faster than I am at least.'

'Bruno says I'm a natural.'

'Where would you do it?'

'There's schools for it – in Wales I think. You can go there for a month and get started.'

'It'll cost a fair bit,' he says. 'Got to be a few grand for training like that and it's only the first step.'

'I'll save up for it,' I tell him. 'Get a job, work evenings, weekends.'

Dad laughs and ruffles my hair a bit. 'We'll see,' he says. 'But maybe it's not such a crazy idea.'

I hurry back through the town and report to the centre one minute before the deadline.

'You look knackered,' Derek says.

He's right. I didn't get much sleep. But I don't care. I'm feeling calm. And sorted. The thing about the rally driving has filled me up with happy juice.

And I know that today I might see *her* again.

61 BECCA

I cross the gangplank, feeling the wood sag beneath my weight. A cat with a cloudy grey coat crosses with me, weaving in and out of my legs and purring like crazy.

Then I see: the door of Mum's boat is sealed with a hefty brass padlock. Blinds have been drawn over the windows.

An elderly man pops his head up in the boat next door.

'You all right, love?'

'I'm looking for Sarah Eden, I tell him. 'This is her boat, isn't it?'

'She's disappeared,' he says. 'Her poor cat's starving half to death.'

'When was the last time you saw her?'

'Forty-eight hours ago. I've had to feed old Phoebe myself.'

'Oh.'

'I'll give it another twenty-four hours,' he says, 'then I'll be calling the police.'

He stares at me with open curiosity for a few moments.

'Not sure I've ever known her have a visitor,' he says. 'Who are you anyway?'

'I'm her daughter,' I tell him. The words come out in a whisper, forced past the housebrick that seems to have lodged in my throat.

'Daughter?' His look turns to outright suspicion. 'I've never heard her mention a *daughter*.'

I turn to go, my cheeks burning.

PART 3
LETHAL AGENT

Patrick Eden: I'm through the washdown room. Pushing deeper into the lab.

Police Command: New update from the backup team. ETA seventeen minutes.

Patrick Eden: I've just entered an animal bay. There's a series of cages here, there are dead monkeys inside. Oh God this is terrible ... terrible.

Audio transcript from helmet mic worn by Patrick Eden, UK Government bioweapons inspector following emergency call at SYMBARON lab, Hampshire.

62 BECCA

The boatman's words have been playing on my mind. Over and over as we head for London and the hospital appointment to check on Dad.

Mum not seen for forty-eight hours. Is she in danger? Did she leave her boat to see Dad? A gnawing core of frustration is rising inside me. Why didn't Dad talk to me about all this?

One thing is clear: I am no longer fighting one battle, I'm fighting two.

Dad's 'suicide'. Mum's disappearance. I need to find the truth about both.

'How did it go back there?' Liz asks. 'Did you get some news about your mum?'

'Not much,' I tell her.

'Really? You sure there's nothing you want to tell me?' Her voice is dripping with suspicion. I catch Liz's eyes in the rear-view mirror. There's a look on her face that I don't really like; the look of an interrogator.

'You should talk to me more,' she says accusingly. I say nothing and before long we are snailing through the London traffic and I'm thinking hard about stuff. Particularly about Liz – the government 'driver' who carries a handgun in a hidden holster. Who *is* she, exactly? And what is her real mission with me?

Yes, she is obviously here for my protection. The press pack would rip me to pieces without her and I definitely appreciate that. But there's a flip side which is starting to make me increasingly uneasy.

She is *controlling* my every move.

63 JOE

I'm back on the wall. I'm on my own. Not even Derek stays to help me out. But I'm not sad to be here. Because ...

There's the watching. The secret watching.

I want to see if that girl comes back. The biologist's daughter.

It's hotter today. Burning sun in July. Hands sweating inside the rubber gloves like slimy slugs.

The chemicals are doing my head in. Got brain ache. Feeling thirsty. Derek said he'd come back and bring me some water but there's no sign of him yet.

As for the graffiti, I'm scrubbing and grinding but there's not too much progress. The Y is almost gone now and I'm getting stuck into the B.

The morning goes by. A whole load of photographers turn up. More than ever. They're hanging about the entrance, chatting with each other. That weird guy with the mirrored shades and the BMW bike cruises slowly past again.

Really I'm just like the press. There's only one thing I'm waiting for. What was her name again? Oh yes ... Rebecca. Out of my league even if I was interested.

Which I'm not. Obviously.

Liz is busy driving. I open up Dad's notebook and start to scan through it.

There's a section titled DARK HEART, with a subtitle VACCINE. Immediately I remember Benson mentioning those same words.

DARK HEART. What can it mean? I see lists of equipment including a centrifuge, a bioreactor, and a pressurised gas container. I flick further through the book, finding page after page of carefully written notes and chemical equations.

'What's in the notebook?' Liz suddenly asks.

'Just a diary,' I tell her.

Her curiosity is a further warning sign. I can't let her get her hands on this book.

'I'll take a look later if that's OK?' she says. There's a hard edge to her tone of voice.

'It's personal stuff,' I tell her. Inside me is a silent scream which says: *get off my back will you?*

'Uh-oh!' Liz exclaims. 'Even more of our press friends are here today.'

An engine roars alongside us. A motorbike is tracking just an arm's length from my window. The passenger is firing off a camera in a series of brilliant flashes. I hold my bag up to hide my face. Ahead of us is the hospital and I see a large crowd of reporters clustered there waiting for us. There are cameramen as well and two policemen are trying to push them back behind a barrier.

'This could get a bit heavy,' Liz says.

I take a deep breath.

65 JOE

As soon as the girl's vehicle arrives, all hell kicks off. Before she's even got out of the car they are pushing and shoving to get their shots.

'Rebecca! Look this way please!'

To my surprise I see that the big guy with the mirrored shades has also joined the pack – a camera in his hand.

'Rebecca! Over here!'

They're jostling against each other. One or two are getting angry. It's all a bit mad.

'Stand away from the car!' The police are trying to keep the snappers back. The girl can't even get out with the guys pressing against her door.

The driver climbs out. I hear her tell Rebecca, 'Stay there for the moment'.

'You need to cool it down a bit,' one of the policemen barks at the paparazzi. 'Someone's going to get hurt if you're not careful.'

'We're on the public highway,' comes the reply. 'What's the big problem?'

The driver wades in with 'Steady now, lads. You don't want to get arrested do you?' and a bit of a scuffle kicks off which ends with one of the video cameras being knocked to the floor.

The cameraman goes crazy, launching a string of swear words at the bloke who nudged him.

Half a second later they are right in each other's faces and it's all flaring up. A punch gets thrown. Then another.

I'm watching out of the window as the fight escalates.

One of the pressmen gets pushed back against the wall. Fists are swinging. A policeman leaps in to try and calm it all down.

Liz steps into the fray. She grabs a wrist in mid-air. Twists an arm behind a back. Suddenly one of the pressmen is on the floor and Liz has her knee in his chest. It happens so fast it takes the whole bunch of them by surprise.

I wind the window down to hear what's happening.

'I don't want to hurt you,' Liz tells the photographer. 'But I will if you don't stop messing around.'

All the fight has gone out of him. Liz lets him stand up and brushes down her suit. The men stare at her with new respect. Even the policemen look a bit awestruck.

I just wish they would leave us in peace. All I want is to get into the hospital to be by Dad's side.

The press people move to the wall, ignoring me for the moment. Then I see graffiti boy standing close by, kind of pretending not to look in my direction. I get a sudden powerful urge to speak to him. I wind the window down a bit more.

'What's happening?' I ask him.

He turns those dark Mediterranean eyes towards me. My heart feels like it's trying to turn itself inside out but I hold his gaze.

67 JOE

We stare at each other for a few seconds and everything goes awkward and quiet. Ten thousand turbocharged butterflies are trying to beat a way out of my chest.

'Camera got smashed,' I tell her. 'Can't say I'm too gutted about it.' Silence again. I have never seen a blue like the blue of her eyes.

'What's your name?' she asks.

'Joe,' I tell her. 'I know your name because you're famous. I'll call you Becca if that's OK?'

Her face blushes bright red. 'Fine,' she says.

'So, what's it like to be a TV star?' I ask her.

'Hell,' she says, smiling. 'I liked my life more when no one was interested.'

'What about that woman, the driver?' I ask. 'What's the deal with her?'

'My personal prison guard,' she says, all the smile vanishing from her face. 'She works for a guy called Benson, basically as a spy. It's a nightmare.'

The driver comes back and pushes me roughly out of the way. 'Come on,' she tells Becca. The press guys start snapping again.

Becca gets out. The men are trying to get their pics. Gradually the pack moves away. Then I notice something: the girl's dropped a notebook – a bright purple one – it's been knocked out of her bag.

Interesting. I pick it up and duck down behind the car to sneak a look.

We're just going through security to get into the hospital. That's when I realise:

'Where's the purple notebook? I was carrying it just now and ... '

I feel a tremor of panic. We start to look around.

No sign. A video camera gets thrust right into my face.

'What's happening?' a reporter asks. 'Did you lose something?'

'It must have fallen out of my bag,' I mutter to Liz.

We search the pavement around the hospital entrance. The reporters join in.

All of my father's research. All the little pieces, the clues that might mean something. Have I lost them?

'Let's go back and look by the car,' I say to Liz. 'It has to be on the ground there.'

'I'll do it,' she snaps. 'You go through security, get out of this mess.'

A guard grabs my arm, pulling me through the gates.

'Wait ... ' I turn.

But the press pack are solid against the security barrier. A furious blast of flashes forces me to step back.

69 JOE

I'm crouched down. Reading. Out of sight.

I hear footsteps running towards me and I sneak a look over the car. Bollocks! The driver's coming! Becca must have realised she's dropped the book.

Then I remember Becca's words, about the driver being a spy and stuff.

What if the driver keeps the book? It's obviously got vital stuff in it. Better I keep it safe, give it back to Becca personally.

There's a police traffic cone behind the car. I ram the notebook right inside, stepping back to the wall just as the minder arrives.

'Have you seen a notebook?' she calls over. I scrub at the graffiti, trying to control my breathing.

'No.'

She checks underneath the motor and looks around the back seat before walking slowly to me. 'You picked it up, didn't you? Where is it?'

I shake my head. She spins me around. 'I think you're lying,' she hisses. 'I'm going to search you.'

I'm shaking as she frisks my body. Finding nothing, she steps across to the police cone and lifts it up. I get a wrenching sensation in my guts. But she just checks underneath the cone and doesn't look up inside it.

'If I find out you've nicked it, you're in serious trouble,' she snaps. Then she walks back to the hospital entrance.

'I can't find it,' Liz says.

'Let me go back and look.'

'I'm telling you it's not there,' she barks.

I turn to the press men. 'Have any of you got my book?' I plead. Dozens of blank faces stare back.

'It's gone,' Liz says. She pulls me into the hospital. A sudden paranoid thought hits me. What if Liz *did* find it and doesn't want to tell me?

Then I wonder if graffiti boy saw something. I have to ask him when I can.

I'm totally stressed now. *Dad's notebook is gone.*

Extreme paranoia grips me. Have I just lost the blueprint to a deadly new bioweapon?

Also, I can't bear the thought that someone else will look through those pages. It's Dad's private possession and I know he wouldn't want anyone but me to have it. My eyes itch with tears and it's all I can do to blink them back.

We climb the stairs. Liz waits in the corridor as I enter Dad's room.

There's still no sign of reaction. Dad remains dead to the world. And I still can't get over that crucifying guilt.

His coma is all my fault.

71 JOE

The driver and Becca have gone into the hospital. And I'm shaking a bit from the aggressive way the driver searched me.

And the close call with the traffic cone.

The snappers wander back. Then I see that one of them – the big guy with those mirrored Ray-Bans – is standing apart, checking out his shots on the little screen on his camera. He's close to me. And I sneak a bit nearer, behind him.

He's lingering on one particular shot. Taken near the hospital entrance but looking back in my direction. He zooms in. Closer. And I see *myself* pictured on his little screen. Picking the notebook up from the floor.

Bummer! If he shows that to the driver I'm in serious trouble.

He turns at that moment. Gives me a weird look. Then a sort of spooky smile.

I try to get back to work. But the big biker in the shades is hanging around and making me nervous. So, even though I want to find a way to give Becca back her notebook as soon as possible, I'm glad when Derek comes early.

After a bit the biker drives off and I get the book out of the traffic cone. I ask Derek to wait but he's got things to do back in the depot so I'm forced to leave before I can give the notebook back.

I'll just have to hand it to Becca tomorrow.

Soon as I get home I find out my front door keys are missing from my bag. How did I lose them? Weird. I can't work it out.

Luckily, Pauline's there to let me in.

The atmosphere in the room is terrible. The duty nurse seems restless and moody. Dad looks thinner and sicker than yesterday, his skin has a yellow tint.

I'm still miserable about the notebook so I do some surfing on my iPad to distract myself. I need to focus: why did someone want Dad dead?

I find plenty of internet references to his early career. He was working as an academic; one of the Cambridge group of outstanding research scientists. The work he did on viruses in those glittering years was reported in academic papers and conference reports from all over the world.

Then came the shift into Ministry of Defence work. I find a couple of references to him at Porton Down, the secretive headquarters of British weapons research, but they are fleeting and obscure.

He moved into the shadows. Became a grey man – a keeper of official secrets. A guardian of information the government does not want the man in the street to know about.

For almost ten years he worked on those projects. Kept quiet about what he knew. Followed the official line. But five days ago his conscience kicked in.

Was the whistle-blower thing motivated by guilt? Had he been personally responsible for creating a deadly new virus? There are so many doubts inside me.

At every stage of his life, Dad was playing with fire.

And last Monday, he finally got his fingers burnt.

PART 4
CAGED TERROR

Patrick Eden: Wait ... two of the monkeys are alive. But they're comatose, bleeding profusely.

Police Command: What infection do they have?

Patrick Eden: I would say some form of filovirus. Marburg, maybe Ebola. But an extreme form. I've never seen anything quite like this. I'm going further into the lab.

Audio transcript from helmet mic worn by Patrick Eden, UK Government bioweapons inspector following emergency call at SYMBARON lab, Hampshire.

73 BECCA

Dad's leap into notoriety as a whistle-blower happened just this week. By chance I was with him that day; he was fulfilling a promise to let me get some work experience with him over the summer holidays.

'I can't take you to the weapons research centre,' Dad had told me. 'I wouldn't get permission. But you could come to the defence trade fair if you like.'

We drove to Farnborough military airfield where a series of huge hangars had been converted into exhibition space. Security was rigorous; I had to bring my passport so it could be photocopied at the entrance.

'You might find this bizarre,' Dad told me. 'It's a bit like the ideal home exhibition at Olympia. Except everything here is about destruction and death.'

He was right; I did find it utterly bizarre. In the very first hangar we saw exhibitors selling armoured vehicles, tanks, rocket launchers and radar tracking systems.

'Last year's trade show generated more than ten billion dollars of sales,' he told me. 'It's the biggest arms fair on the planet.'

A delegation of Arab dignitaries swept past, dressed in flowing robes and headdresses.

'That's the defence minister of Saudi Arabia,' my father muttered.

'What about those?' I asked him. We were looking at a company stand: BIO CONTROL SYSTEMS. Their table was laden with these matt-black metal canisters.

'Landmines. Cluster bombs,' he said.

'What are the rules about this?' I asked him. 'Can *anyone* buy these things?'

'Pretty much,' he told me. 'There are nations that are banned because their human rights record is dodgy but it's a joke really, they can easily buy through intermediaries.'

I felt a shiver of revulsion run through me. It all just felt so wrong. For a few hundred dollars you could buy a device that would kill and maim dozens of people.

'Did you ever design these types of things?' I asked him.

A little voice was whispering urgently in my ear, 'Please say no. Just say no.'

'Never. And my work is diagnostic these days, Becks. Analysing bioweapons so the government can keep up to date with what our enemies are doing. I'm more at the inspection end of things.'

His words came as a relief. But seeds of doubt had always been inside me.

In the afternoon the prime minister flew in. He was meeting various foreign VIPs and having a few words with defence journalists. It was thrilling to see his helicopter land, take my seat next to Dad in the hushed auditorium.

'A warm welcome to you all,' the prime minister said. 'It's wonderful to see representatives here from just about every nation on earth, celebrating the UK's role as a leading manufacturer of defence technology.'

He kept the speech short and then took a few questions from the journalists. Nothing challenging cropped up until a nervy young reporter sitting close to us put up his hand.

'I have a question regarding the death of the scientist Simon Hazelgrove last week, prime minister. The official cause of death has been given as accidental exposure to toxic gas, but rumours are spreading that he might actually have died from a new form of the Ebola virus. Have you got any comment on that, sir?'

The room went deathly quiet. Dad was shifting uncomfortably in his seat. The prime minister coughed into his handkerchief. Seconds later he recovered his composure, uttering a denial and some vague words about Britain's commitment to transparency when it came to disclosures about bioweapon threats to the public.

But the journalist wasn't giving up.

'It's also becoming clear, prime minister, that the government has no idea at all who was actually funding this unlicensed, illegal research laboratory. It seems the web of banks and offshore trusts paying for it was too elaborate to pin down an actual backer beyond some vague links to a shadowy warlord in Kazakhstan. Is that true, sir?'

The prime minister glanced to the wings of the stage. It was almost like he was looking for a prompt from his advisors.

'The lab in question was established using virtual currencies,' he said hesitantly. 'Cryptocurrencies. The payments are literally impossible to trace. This is one of the new threats we have to deal with; Bitcoin, Litecoin, Dogecoin, Peercoin, Primecoin. The laboratory was paid for in a way that the owners can be totally anonymous. Now, if you'll excuse me, I have other meetings to attend.'

As his aides swept the prime minister from the room, Dad turned to the journalist and, without making any attempt to keep his voice down, said, 'Simon Hazelgrove didn't die from accidental exposure to gas. I'm one of the team that found him so I know that for sure.'

I felt my whole body chill.

'Are you saying the prime minister is lying?' the journalist replied.

'I ... er ... '

'Dad, let's go.' I clutched his hand, pulled him away.

But we didn't get far. Within seconds a handful of journalists were gathered around us, all firing questions.

'What more can you tell us about Simon Hazelgrove's death, Mr Eden?'

'Why has it taken so long for the results of the autopsy to be released?'

'Is it true that video footage exists of his death, Mr Eden?'

We burst out of the hall, almost at a run. As we got to the car park a camera crew joined the throng.

Dad hit the accelerator like the devil was on our tail. He wheelspun out of the muddy car park faster than I had ever known him drive before, almost sideswiping a security guard as we shook off the journalists.

Things deteriorated fast from that point. Dad's boss Marcus Benson was waiting for us when we got home. Dad disappeared into his office with him and their raised voices could be heard all over the house. I wasn't trying to eavesdrop but the conversation got so heated I couldn't avoid hearing it.

'You know you could go to jail for this!' I heard Benson cry at one point. 'You've broken the Official Secrets Act.'

'Tell me what the tests revealed,' Dad protested. 'Don't you think the British public deserve to know?'

That was Monday. The press were calling our home phone number non-stop even though Dad answered every enquiry with 'no comment'. In the end he took the phone off the hook.

On Tuesday morning the *Daily Mail* had a photograph of Dad on the front page alongside the headline 'Whistle-blower'. Dad came home early from work that day, his face white with worry.

'They changed the locks on my office,' he told me. 'I've been told to take some time off.'

Then, with breathtaking speed, the lies and smears began.

It began with an unnamed government source. A revelation that documents had been found amongst Dad's papers linking him to 'organisations with known terrorist links'.

'It's my job to inspect those organisations,' Dad told me miserably. 'They're trying to scare me into silence.'

Other forms of negative publicity came thick and fast in the next forty-eight hours. An accusation of marijuana use during Dad's university years. An 'exclusive' in the *Daily Mirror* about a night in the cells and a police caution at Oxford after an undergraduate party got out of hand.

'It was one of those stupid student pranks,' Dad told me. 'We were celebrating the end of exams and we parked a lecturer's car in the river as a joke.'

It was character assassination, pure and simple.

In just three days, through online news sites, gossip forums, mainstream press and radio, Dad's name was blackened, dragged through the mud.

On Thursday morning we were having breakfast together. Dad was restless, there were dark rings under his eyes.

'I'm going to see Simon Hazelgrove's widow today,' he said. 'Talk to her and his daughter Cora, see if they can shine any light on what he was doing.'

'I didn't know he had a daughter.'

'Yes. She's eighteen.'

'Oh.' I felt a strong stab of pity for her.

Then I asked the question I'd been wanting to ask ever since the trip to the trade fair:

'Dad? How did Hazelgrove die? What really killed him?'

'That's what I need to find out,' he whispered. 'I'm afraid it was some sort of super pathogen. Something incredibly fast and virulent.'

'Super pathogen?'

'Combining the genes of two pathogens – it's a means of weaponisation. In this case I fear we are talking about Ebola and an airborne disease such as anthrax. The combination of those two would be so infectious it would spread like wildfire. Kill with incredible speed.'

'Why would he do that? Was he crazy? Evil? How well did you know him?'

'He was a colleague for years. But the pressure of work got to him. He had a nervous breakdown and got sacked from Defence HQ about four years ago. For a long time he was un-employed but this private laboratory must have recognised his potential and given him a free rein to experiment. It's possi-ble he thought he was working for a legitimate organisation.'

Later I was tidying up some weeds in the vegetable garden. Dad came to join me but he was distracted and moody and I felt like I was walking on eggshells.

He worked for a while then managed to pull up a whole row of strawberry plants by mistake.

'Damn it!' he yelled. He snatched up a rake and ran across the lawn to the greenhouse. He raised the rake above his head and began to break the panes of glass, smashing them one after the other with this manic gleam in his eye.

I stood there, wide-eyed, waiting for him to stop.

Then he threw down the rake and walked away.

Dad got some new lab equipment delivered on the Thursday. I wanted to help him with whatever he was planning but he told me to take Arcturus for a ride. Later he disappeared from the house and when he got home at ten that evening he looked more grave than I had ever seen him.

He said nothing to me that night, just retreated to his office where I heard him talking agitatedly on the phone.

The next morning was Friday and the 'suicide' attempt. I thought it was the week from hell.

But what is happening now is far, far worse.

74 JOE

I make myself a cup of tea and take it up to my room. I open the notebook. I feel well guilty that I've still got it but I really want to suss that girl out before I give it back. Want to try and get into her head. 'Specially now.

But the truth is this: I don't understand what I'm seeing. There's plenty of formulas and biological data. But actual words? Not too many. One thing leaps out though, DARK HEART. I wonder if it's a kind of code name.

I flick through the pages wondering what it's all about? Weapons using horrific diseases? Secret nerve agents, viruses that are genetically modified to be extra lethal? That's what the papers are saying.

It's definitely scary.

But *she* must understand all this. Must be able to work it out. Which makes her a different creature. From a different planet. With some sort of wiring in her brain that makes her a genius. And that's when I give her a nickname. There is only one nickname that does the business:

Little Miss Einstein.

At the back of the notebook I find a scribbled line in what must be Little Miss E's writing.

Check out Ebola. Infection percentage rates? Time to death?

I borrow Pauline's laptop and google *Ebola*. After fifteen minutes or so I'm feeling totally sick.

Ebola is a terrible way to die.

75 BECCA

I give Dad a kiss on the cheek. I acknowledge the nurse's mumbled goodbye.

Back at the car I see that graffiti boy has gone. There's no sign of the notebook.

We arrive home at 6 p.m. Benson and his forensic team are still poking around the house, looking for clues.

I can't bear being in the house with them so I go straight to the stables. Arcturus nuzzles me a greeting and I'm happy to see he's clean and well looked after. The farmer next door has been a real star, stepping in to care for him.

I saddle him up and we take a gentle twenty-minute ride through the fields. He's nervy, still sensing that something has changed, but the ride bonds us back together in a good way, even if it is distracting to have Liz following us on a quad bike. Normally we end with a crazy gallop through the woods but today I just keep him on a tight rein and take it easy.

I wash Arcturus down, taking pleasure in the ritual. Then a voice interrupts me. 'Did you have a good ride, Rebecca?' It's Benson. Watching me work.

'I've got something for you,' he says. He reaches in his pocket and hands me my mobile.

'It's curious how few friends you have,' he continues. 'Girls your age would normally be tweeting and WhatsApping their friends non-stop wouldn't they? Your phone is something of a void.'

I say nothing, praying he will not notice my reddening cheeks; the way my hand has clenched into a fist.

'I thought we might resume our little chat about your father and his work,' he says. 'Pick up where we left off the other day.'

My heart sinks. Why won't he leave me alone?

76 JOE

Ebola came from Africa, I discover, an ancient virus from the jungles of Zaire.

Normally it's found in fruit bats and monkeys but somewhere along the line it switched to people, jumping from one victim to another through body fluids.

When you get infected you are in for a roller-coaster horror ride.

First comes fever and this savage pain in the temples. The muscles in your face go droopy and your eyeballs turn crimson red. Your whole body gets covered in this vicious red and black rash and you get angry and aggressive like you want to kill the world.

I turn away from the laptop. Take a deep breath. I don't want to read on but somehow I have to.

Then comes what they call *Vomito Negro*, the stage when you are literally sicking up this black and red slimy goo for hours on end. Most of it is your dissolved flesh and internal bits like your kidneys and liver and stuff.

Finally you start to bleed out of every single orifice in your body.

The nastiest type of Ebola kills ninety per cent of its victims.

I find a couple of websites that say Ebola bioweapons are only a matter of time. Did Little Miss E's dad invent something like that? Is that why someone wanted to kill him?

Then the balloon pops and I get a big smack of **guilt** about what I'm doing. Little Miss E must be slammed to have lost this notebook. Maybe I should have waited longer at the hospital today, made more effort to get it back to her.

Anyway, I *will* give it back to her. As soon as I can.

'Your father must have had a secret laboratory,' Benson says. His eyes bore into me. 'Are we right, Rebecca? Is there somewhere he did his personal projects?'

A powerful conflict kicks off inside me. To lie to him, or to anyone in fact, goes against everything my parents ever taught me. It goes against everything that I *am*.

'Tell me, Rebecca,' he says urgently. 'Time is running out. I already told you he removed samples illegally from our research centre so he had to be analysing them somewhere.'

I stare at him. And I realise something fundamental: I don't trust this man.

'I've never heard him mention any sort of special lab,' I tell Benson, looking him right in the eye. 'I can't help you.'

Benson gathers his team together and, after searching the house one more time, they drive away. I'm left with Liz and the police security team.

I'm satisfied they have gone. But I'm so sad that I have had to lie. It feels like I just broke a precious part of myself. At the same moment Dad's words come back to haunt me.

Lie. Kill. Walk away. Maybe I am no better than them.

But at least I know what I have to do now.

The Ice House.

The hidden laboratory. Regardless of the risk, I *must* go to the Ice House tonight.

It's evening. I take Shammy to the park for his last walk of the day. I'm still shaken up about that Ebola stuff so it's a good distraction to watch him running around and having some fun. Sometimes I think he likes his night walk the best. Not so many other big dogs around.

Shammy still likes people. Even after what happened to him before.

We go to a late store and I get him some liquorice. He loves it for some reason. When we get back, Dad and Pauline are just going out for drinks and supper at the club. Dad asks me if I want to come so we lock up Shammy in the house and off we go.

The club is packed out. There's music on the jukebox.

Dad's in one of his good moods. Messing about and doing that thing where you flip up the beer mats and catch them. He can do twenty, his hands are that big. I can do ten. Well, I did once.

'I did some research today,' he says.

'Yeah?'

'About the rally thing.'

I get a good feeling when I hear those words. I just knew Dad would back me up on this one.

'There's a rally school up in Northampton,' he goes on. 'Why don't I buy you a try-out session as a little reward for ditching your paints? See if you're any good? It's all on private forest tracks so you don't need to be seventeen.'

Yes!

79 BECCA

I wait impatiently as the house settles into night mode. Two-hundred-year-old oak beams stretching and yawning as they prepare to sleep.

I ponder on Benson's words as I lie there: his disturbing comment about Dad taking samples from the government lab.

What samples? Why would Dad break the rules like that? Was Benson talking about Ebola? Is that why Dad made so many references to Ebola in the notebook, which I have now managed to lose?

There's still a hundred questions needing an answer.

Did Simon Hazelgrove invent some sort of super pathogen in that illegal lab? And who was behind the lab anyway? What was their master plan before it went so horribly wrong?

No wonder the government are so desperate to keep it all quiet. There would be panic in the streets if people thought Ebola was about to strike.

Half an hour later I push my bedroom door open and pad quietly to the top of the stairs. Once I am there I stand for a full couple of minutes in absolute silence. No one is stirring. I can hear Liz snoring gently in her room.

I make it down the stairs, cross to the window and gently pull back the curtain. The policemen are out there – two of them, chatting in the front seat of a patrol car.

A shiver runs through my body. I have no idea what they will do if they catch me trying to leave the house. I could still be discovered at any moment.

80 JOE

I'm made up about Dad's news. All we have to do is book the session and I'll be climbing into a real rally car! Pulling out on to a forest track. With a pro by my side to help me learn.

Me. Joe Fontana. It's almost unbelievable really.

'Thanks Dad,' I tell him. I really want to give him a hug but I know he won't appreciate it here in the club.

We chat about it a bit more. Then Dad says he's off on another run up to Norwich for diesel. Pauline says she's going to see her mum, so I'm away on my own through the dark streets back home. Hoping I don't bump into any of the gangs.

As soon as I get in there's this terrible smell, like someone's been sick. Everything is strangely quiet.

Then I notice something that doesn't make sense: there's a bit of meat, like the end of a sausage or something, lying on the hallway floor. Why's it there?

Shamrock should be here, jumping up and yapping away. Goosebumps ripple along my arms. Then I hear it: a small whining noise from the kitchen.

I walk slowly down the corridor, heading for the kitchen door.

The policemen are still talking in the car. I let the curtain fall back in place and move stealthily through the kitchen and into the utility room at the back.

Two minutes later I am out into the cool night air of the garden.

There's a beech hedge there, dividing our land from the farmer next door. I push through it. There's a few young cows grazing in the moonlight but luckily they don't bellow or start stampeding around.

I make my way down the field, cross a stile, then I'm back into the copse for the first time since the incident.

Through the trees, I can make out a flickering paraffin lamp. I see the silhouettes of two more policemen, guarding the forensics tent, which has been erected over the crime scene. My breathing quickens. I focus hard, trying to control the fear.

I creep towards the southern edge of the copse, weaving a wary trail through the trees. Here, cut into the side of the valley, is the amphitheatre shape of the old quarry.

And an innocent-looking tumbledown summer house set against the rock.

Hidden behind that summer house is Dad's secret world – a world that, it now occurs to me, he had been subtly discouraging me to visit in recent days.

Shamrock. Lying on the kitchen floor. He's twitching and his eyes are rolling about. His fur's all wet with stuff. He's been sick everywhere.

He doesn't raise his head He doesn't even try to lick my hand. I stroke him.

What's happened? Why is he so ill? Thoughts of those Ebola victims flash crazily in my mind.

Then I think about the vets we take Shammy to for his injections and everything. Last time we were there I noticed a sticker with a twenty-four-hour emergency number.

It might cost a packet but it has to be worth a try.

I rush upstairs and get a towel from the bathroom to wrap him in. I pick him up and he's heavier than I thought.

Then I'm out into the night and running for the vets with Shamrock in my arms. It's about ten minutes of jogging and he just gets heavier and heavier.

He looks so bad, I think he's going to die. I've got this terrible stabbing pain in my head just at the thought of it.

The clinic is completely shut, but I call the emergency number next to the door then wait with Shammy trembling in my arms before the vet drives up.

She takes one look at Shamrock and says, 'This dog is extremely sick. Bring him in.'

83 BECCA

Up until six or seven years ago the Ice House was just a forgotten curiosity of the garden. It's a man-made cave, chiselled out of the rock. You could play a good game of badminton in there, that's how big it is.

Dad reckons it was a cold-storage place in the days before fridges.

One day, he came up with this wonderful idea: his workroom in the house had been growing every year and he was running out of space. Then he thought about the Ice House and he equipped it as a fully fledged laboratory.

'My own personal bat cave!' I remember Dad laughing as he put the finishing touches to the job, installing power and lights.

Then he bought this wooden summer house and erected it in front of the entrance. It fitted perfectly. You'd never know what was behind.

Inside the summer house he built a secret door. It was a clever piece of work – just about invisible.

I feel for the little steel catch that holds the door in place. I swing it open and enter the chilled interior of the cave. I close the door behind me as quietly as I can.

And I turn on the light.

The vet takes Shammy into a little room.

Ten minutes later she comes out. I can see from her face it's not going to work out.

She gets me into the room. There is Shamrock, lying on this white cloth and he looks lost and screwed up and dirty all over.

'I'm sorry to have to tell you this,' she tells me. 'He's been poisoned and his kidneys are failing. I'm going to have to put him down.'

Put him down? Oh Shammy!

'There's no choice?' I ask her urgently. 'What if he has an operation?'

'I'm afraid it's too late. Whatever poison he's eaten has left him in a critical condition. If he regained consciousness he would be in terrible pain.'

'It's not Ebola is it?' I feel my cheeks burning up, I feel so stupid to say it.

She stares in surprise. 'Ebola? No. It's some sort of rat poison I think.'

I can't stop the tears now. The vet gives me a tissue.

'Do you know who might have done it?' she asks.

I rub at my eyes but the tears just won't stop.

'No. I just came home and there he was.'

'Hmmm.' She looks at me oddly. 'Well someone must know what he's eaten and that person's likely to be in trouble with the police if it's found to be deliberate.'

85 BECCA

Trashed.

There is no other word for it. Dad's secret laboratory has been *trashed*. Annihilated. With extreme violence.

I look around the scene, hardly able to take it in. The benches of instruments destroyed. The reference books ripped up. Every single square inch of floorspace filled with an unholy chaos of crunched-up debris.

I move further into the cave, picking out details of this extraordinary mess. My eyes swim with tears. Dad's world, wrecked.

Electronic components have been crushed. Cables and wires have been scattered to the corners of the cave. Chips and processors have been clawed from their motherboards.

Then the hairs on the back of my head stand up on end. I hear a noise.

At least I *think* I hear a noise. It's a metallic sort of click. Followed by an incredibly quiet hiss, which sounds like compressed air moving through a tube.

The noise comes from the smaller room that has been hacked out of the back of the cave. The place where they used to hang meat.

I move towards it, wondering what on earth I am going to find.

86 JOE

'Do you want to leave?' she says. 'I promise he won't feel a thing.'

'No. I'll stay.' I breathe in hard. Trying to stay in control but my whole body's trembling.

I stroke Shamrock's head while the vet gets some metal things from a drawer. He's still got his eyes open but they're all milky and there's this dribble coming from his mouth.

I take another tissue out of the box and wipe it up. There's this cracking noise as she breaks open a plastic tube. Then she gets a syringe. Fills it up with plenty of the stuff.

She puts the needle into the top of his leg. The fluid goes in. It takes longer than I think. I'm biting, hard, against my lip.

'Shouldn't be long now,' she says.

Shamrock starts shivering a bit. He's panting in a heavy way and his legs are jerking.

'There we are,' says the vet. She's stroking his fur. 'You're all right, boy.'

And I have to close my eyes. Cos I don't want to see the end. He's the only dog I've ever had. My best friend, really. I hear a sort of gasp from him.

Then the jerking stops.

In the back room of the Ice House I find the most extraordinary thing: a huge polished metal door has been built into the rock. A metal door that looks like it could survive a nuclear explosion, it is so heavily made.

Could this have been where the sound came from? Is some experiment going on inside it?

The metal looks like titanium. A handwritten sign has been stuck to it. It reads:
ATTEMPTING TO OPEN THIS DOOR WITH
OXYACETYLENE OR OTHER CUTTING EQUIPMENT
WILL TRIGGER SEMTEX PROTECTION DEVICE.

Semtex? A type of plastic explosive. I stare at the sign in shock. The door is booby trapped with explosives? Why would Dad do that?

I realise there is no handle. Instead I see a polished chrome entry pad with twelve black ceramic buttons. Then I notice that each of the ceramics has a symbol etched into it. I find a pencil and a scrap of paper on the floor and copy the symbols down.

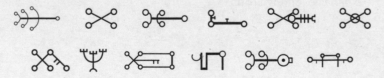

Then the noise happens *again*. Another almost inaudible hiss.

And now I'm really freaked. What *is* going on behind that door?

88 JOE

I open my eyes, seeing him through a shimmering blur of tears. The vet hands me another tissue, the first one's soaked through.

'I'm going to run some tests,' she tells me gently. 'Try to find out what type of poison he ate. Is that all right?'

'Yeah,' I say through gritted teeth. 'Find out. I want to catch them.'

So. That's it. The end of Shamrock. And I'm walking home through the midnight streets, legs wobbly with the shock of it all, and I'm thinking:

Who would want to poison Shamrock? And why?

I think about my dad. Pauline says there's people who are after him. People who want to take over Bruno's diesel business. Like the mafia or something. Maybe someone had a go at Shamrock as a warning.

Doesn't sound likely to me. If they want to have a go at my dad then they'll target *him*. Not my dog.

I'm thinking we'll have to tell the police. That's the last thing I want. But otherwise they'll get away with it. Daylight murder.

Then, as I get close to home, I have a new idea. That poisoner might think they're pretty smart. But I'm not so dumb myself. Because what they don't know is this: there might be video of them doing it.

And *I* might be able to get it.

Next to the metal door I see a word chalked on to the rock wall.

FIZZES.

Fizzes? What's that about? It looks like one of Dad's cryptic codes.

Another noise comes from inside the vault. This time a scratching sound.

I have to get out of this place. Half panicking, I rush back to the entrance, turn off the lights and close the Ice House shut.

As I step out into the little quarry I see something flickering in the distance. There are lights on in the upstairs floor of the house. I have to get back fast!

'Rebecca!' Liz shouts my name into the night. She sounds furious.

I race through the copse as fast as I dare. Thorns are tugging at my hair as I push my way through.

I hear another shout. Liz has alerted the two armed police officers and their footsteps are now pounding on the gravel of the driveway.

I cross into the field. The cattle are kicking and bucking in alarm. Through the top floor window I see the policemen start their search upstairs. What to do? No choice. I just have to front this one out.

I make it to the back door just as Liz appears.

She has a gun in her hand.

90 JOE

I have to move quickly on this video thing. Right now. Tonight. Or it might get taped over. Where is it? I'll tell you.

Across the road from our house is this late night convenience store. The bloke who owns it is Mr Nasim. Sells food, cigarettes, sweets, hot sausage rolls from a little cooker thing. There's always kids hanging round there. Sometimes he's open until one or two in the morning.

What happened was Mr Nasim had some trouble. Some local idiots bricked his window.

So what Mr Nasim did was buy a CCTV camera. And he was smart about it. Kept it quiet. It was a small one. Hidden in the cigarette rack behind him. You could hardly see it. But it pointed right at the window. I knew about it because I was doing a paper round for him to get some cash.

It got the result. The kids bricked his window again as soon as it was fixed and they were done on the video evidence.

So far as I know that camera's still going. Twenty-four hours a day. *And*, if he hasn't moved it, you can see right across the street.

Our front door is in the bottom right-hand corner of the picture.

'What on earth do you think you're doing?' Liz hisses at me. Her eyes are as sharp and cold as flint.

The two policemen run into the hallway.

'Nothing,' I gabble. 'I couldn't sleep. Went out to the garden to think ... '

The three of them stare at me as if I am absolutely stark raving mad.

'Have you any idea how dangerous that could be?' Liz snaps. 'Lurking around the back of this house in dark clothing? With these guys around? You could have been shot.'

I stare at my feet, feeling like a four-year-old getting a ticking off.

'Get back upstairs,' Liz tells me. She follows me up there and makes sure I go to my room. 'Now go to sleep. And don't mess me around any more. All right?'

I climb into bed and lie there with all senses running at some absurd level of heightened stress. Thinking about the discovery in the Ice House.

Who destroyed the lab? And what is happening behind that strange door cut into the rock? And what about the symbols? They have to contain a hidden code that will open that door. I need to check those symbols out and I need to do it right now.

I find a torch, slip under the covers, and open the sheet of paper.

I tell Mr Nasim about Shammy and he's well angry about it.

'Some people are the limit,' he says.

He agrees to let me check the video.

He rewinds the security tape for me and leaves me to it. The picture is black and white and a bit flickery but it does the job. After a bit I find the place where me and Dad and Pauline leave the house to go to the club.

Then, at 9.15 on the timecode, a motorbike pulls up outside the house. I recognise the bike and I recognise him – it's the guy in the mirrored shades that hangs around at the hospital!

A big fist of fury gets balled up in my belly. I thought he was dodgy, but this … ?

He walks up to the house and he slips something inside the letterbox. The poison. Then he goes back to his bike and rides off.

Ten minutes later on the tape he comes back. This time he looks more nervy.

He walks up to the door. He's got a small bag on his back. He opens the door with a key.

What the … ?

Then I get it. He's got *my* key to the front door – the key I lost back at the wall. He must have stolen it out of my bag while I was scrubbing the graffiti. Then followed me home to see where I lived.

My whole body goes rigid.

Now. *What about these signs?* I stare at them intently for a few minutes thinking I might get a Eureka moment.

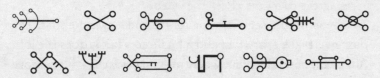

No Eureka moment. I really have no idea. A candelabra? An elephant? Circles and lines. Not a clue. OK. So, first things first. I need to make some assumptions before I can start. So I write down the following:

First assumption: The signs have to have a logical order.

Second assumption: that logical order must relate to a code that opens the door. Is the word on the wall connected? FIZZES. And if so ... how?

I stare at the signs for a while. Trying to think like Dad would think. Trying to imagine what the significance of these weird symbols could be.

OK. Back to basics. What do I know they are *not*?

Well they are nothing to do with the elements. Those symbols are completely different. I can't think of any branch of chemistry which would involve symbols like this. Nor of any aspect of physics. And they don't come from space science.

What *are* they? And what is the FIZZES connection?

I *have* to crack the code to stand any chance of getting that door open.

I thank Mr Nasim and I go back home.

I run up to my room and look underneath the little cupboard in the corner.

The notebook is gone. Little Miss Einstein's vital notebook. That's what the Dog Poisoner came for.

In all the sadness and anger of the Shammy thing I'd forgotten I even had it. But that's the connection. That's why Shamrock died. Because the Dog Poisoner, whoever he is, wanted that notebook.

And it's a sickener. A total sickener, because now I know that if I hadn't been so stupid as to keep hold of the notebook then Shammy wouldn't be dead.

And I've let Becca down, big time. All her Dad's secrets gone.

Sometimes I could hate my own guts. And I've got no idea what I should do about all this.

I lie there for a bit, just feeling like crap. Then I turn to the photo. The special one of me and Mum on the beach.

And I just want to ask her how I can find a way through this mess. I know she'd understand much better than Dad. If she was still here.

I pick the photo up and lie back on the bed to look more closely at it. A whole load of memories about Mum come flooding into my head. Some that I want. And some that I don't want at all. And one day that I know I'll never forget.

As long as I live.

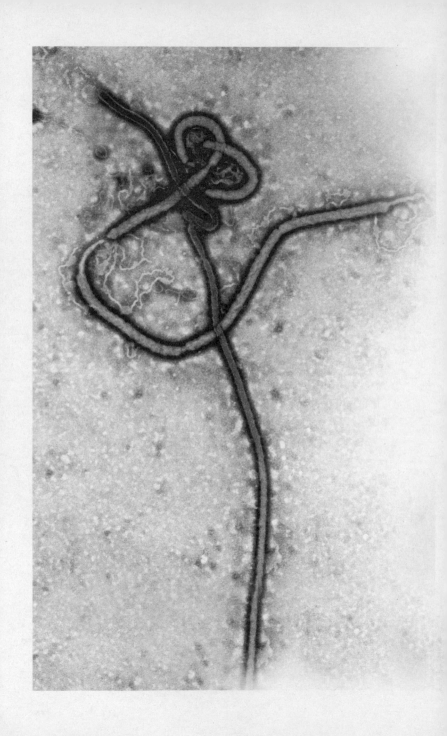

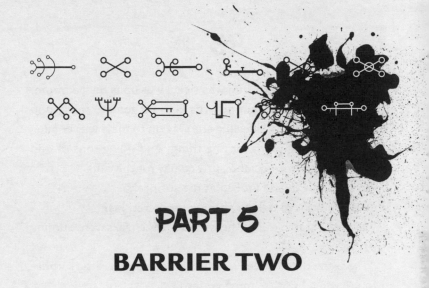

PART 5
BARRIER TWO

Patrick Eden: I've reached a metal seal. Stronger than before.

Police Command: You've gone far enough. Come out now Dr Eden, wait for the backup to arrive.

Patrick Eden: I need to find him. I'm spinning this lock open now. I'm going in deeper.

Audio transcript from helmet mic worn by Patrick Eden, UK Government bioweapons inspector following emergency call at SYMBARON lab, Hampshire.

95 JOE

Back in the day, when Mum was sick, I was up in my bedroom. It was about three or four months after I'd got into the graffiti and I had this horrible feeling she was on to me. I was coming in stinking of the paint for one thing. And doing tons of odd jobs and paper rounds and stuff to pay for the cans.

So she came in and looked at me strangely.

'Do you want to tell me about your secret, Joe?'

'Secret?' I stared out of the window. My cheeks were burning up.

'The secret that's under your bed,' she said. 'The little surprise I found when I was cleaning yesterday.'

I felt the room spin a bit because I knew if Dad got involved then it could get heavy.

Then she got down on the floor and pulled the bag out. And she was smiling while she did it.

'That's none of your business!' I told her. I grabbed hold of the bag and we sort of wrestled with it for a second or two, but we were laughing not angry. Then her wig fell half off and that made her get even more hysterics.

She could always laugh, my Mum. Even with the chemo and everything.

She put the wig right and flopped on the bed. Then she un-zipped the bag, bringing out some of my cans and checking them out.

'Amazing names,' she said with a smile. 'Smoothie, Ozone, Iceberg, Flirt.'

'Yeah, you get to know the colours after a while.'

'Where do you do it?'

'Anywhere. You won't tell Dad will you?'

'Course not,' she said. 'I just want to see what you've done, Joe.

I never thought of my boy as an artist. Why don't you take me on a bit of a tour?'

'*Really?*' I was totally gobsmacked. But she wasn't messing about; she really did want to see my work.

I got Mum wrapped up in her scarves and gloves. She was in the middle of a treatment and it was dangerous for her to get cold.

'Bring your paints,' she said. She had this mischievous look. I still half suspected she was going to tell me to dump them.

Then we walked down to this abandoned office block where I'd laid down some of my early stuff. We had to be careful because the floor was covered in crunchy glass with the odd needle here and there.

'That was the first one I did,' I told her. It was purple and grey and green, interlocking letters, about five metres wide. The position was quite good, on a wall in the old canteen, at the top of a half-wrecked staircase.

She looked up. Her eyes went kind of watery.

'SHAM,' she read. 'Isn't that what it says?'

'Yeah. That's my ident. I sprayed that one just after I picked him up from the dogs' home.'

'That's fantastic, Joe!' Mum grabbed my hand so tight, I thought she was going to crush my fingers. 'You really have a talent for it!'

We saw a few more. A couple on the side of the railway wall. My biggest one – seven metres wide, three metres high, down on the canal bridge.

'Did you know I used to love art at school?' Mum said.

'No.' I wasn't surprised though. Mum was good at everything really, she just never made a big deal out of it.

'I even wanted to go to college and study it,' she went on. 'But certain other beautiful things happened at that time.'

She put her arm around my shoulder and squeezed hard. I knew what she meant because she had me really young, only eighteen.

'So how about you lend me a bit of your paint,' she said, 'and I'll do some graffiti for *you*!'

'What?' I remember my face started aching I was smiling so much.

'Do you know a place, Joe? Somewhere special?'

As it happened, I did. A nice bit of wall separating the sports centre from the park, a quiet place away from the crowds where no other taggers had been. I'd been saving it for something important so this was ideal. Ten minutes later we were there and she was unzipping the bag and giving a can a shake.

'You want me to help you?' I asked her.

She gave me a look. And started to work.

At first I thought she was doing a heart. A broad sweep of her arm stretching full length with a nicely even line of dark brown. But then she repeated the same shape on the other side and I realised what it was.

A butterfly.

'You've been planning this!' I told her.

'Maybe!' she laughed.

Then she started on the colours, creating a burst of lines spreading outwards from the butterfly's body. It was like this incredible rainbow and it was awesome.

Before long she was spraying the last bits of the butterfly. Swirling pinks and green. A really good starburst of bright yellow as a dot in the middle of each wing.

Then she said something really quiet and gentle.

'I'm not going to make it, Joe.'

And the cans were still hissing. She was doing the antennae at the top. Switched to dark blue and grey. And I tried to focus on the way her arm was moving, very graceful and clever.

'You understand what I mean by that, don't you? I've told them to stop the treatment, Joe. I can't take any more.'

She picked up the can of black. Laid in some shadow along the side of the butterfly's wings. Giving it real depth. Dark, dark shadow.

And I just said, 'Oh.' I felt so dizzy I looked round for a place to sit down.

'All done.' She packed the cans up in the bag. 'What do you think?'

And it really was beautiful. But I was all kind of frozen up with what she'd just said, so I couldn't say a thing.

We walked over to a park bench and sat down side by side.

'Come,' she said. And she pulled me towards her so that her arm was around me and my head was resting against her shoulder. And there weren't any tears because this was beyond tears. It was beyond everything.

'I'm so proud of you Joe,' she said. 'You make me proud later, won't you? After I've gone?'

She kissed the top of my head.

It was getting a bit cold. The end of the day. So we took one last look at the butterfly and I suddenly thought of something.

'You should put your tag. Just a small one. Put your name if you like.'

And Mum thought a bit, then she pulled out the yellow and sprayed JILU in tiny letters to the side of the butterfly.

'JILU?' I asked her. 'What's that?'

'Joe I love you,' she said.

The butterfly is still there. And so is the JILU tag. I go down there a lot to check no one's painted over it.

And no one has.

I reach for my iPad and get online, listening out all the while for the sound of Liz coming back up the stairs.

So what's the conclusion? These weird signs definitely look *scientific*. But I *am* a student of science and I have never seen them before.

So if they are not *scientific* what are they? Then I get a break-through thought. Maybe they are *pseudo* scientific. They *do* look like the sort of things you'd see on a cranky old wizard's cloak in a film.

Fifteen minutes online gets me there. At a website devoted to medieval astrology I find a reference to the symbols of fifteen stars considered useful for magical applications.

They are called the *Behenian Fixed Stars*.

I enter these words into Google and a few seconds later I am there. That's what they are.

I turn off the iPad and switch off the torch. I have no more strength now and I resolve to try and crack the order another day. One thing is for sure. I have to get that metal door open as soon as possible.

What will be inside? Will it be the illegal sample that Benson is talking about?

I am hyper-exhausted. I feel like I will never sleep again. And that's a good time for personal demons to come and play. I lie there awake; Benson's words about my lack of friends are still stinging. I'm sure he was just goading me, trying to make me crack, but what he was saying was true.

The fact is I had plenty of friends up to the age of ten. Then everything changed.

It was late autumn when Mum came back from hospital.

She had been away for three months and my hugs and kisses of welcome were blanked in a most callous way. Dad saw my distress but retreated into his shell. Emotional confrontation really wasn't his thing.

Next morning I came down and found her in the kitchen. She was on her knees on the tiled floor, scrubbing at the wall next to the pantry. She whirled abruptly as I entered and I could see her eyes were glazed, her neck shiny with perspiration.

'Such a mess,' she told me accusingly. 'The wall's almost ruined.'

She got back to it, her right arm moving in tight, aggressive little circles, the sharp sound of the bristles setting my teeth on edge.

I walked slowly towards her. I was sleepy and confused. I didn't understand why she seemed angry with me. It took me a few moments for my young mind to really comprehend what she was doing.

Then I saw. She was cleaning the marks off the wall.

The ink scrawls and felt-tip scribbles, the lines and dates and silly exclamation marks that recorded my height over the months and years of my life. Right from the time I first stood on my own two feet at the age of fourteen months.

'The biro ones are the worst,' she muttered. 'Almost impossible.'

She dipped the brush again and again into soapy water, ferocious in her determination to get that wall spotless.

I stood with my mouth open, watching the tiny lines and comments disappear. The place where Dad had written FIRST TOOTH at toddler height. The RODE BICYCLE

WITHOUT STABILISERS a little bit higher. And, in my mother's handwriting, 7 YEARS OLD TODAY! HAPPY BIRTHDAY DARLING!

1m 27cms.

Higher and higher she went, the wall running with blue, black, red ink until the whole thing was a mess of dark grey foam. Specks were flying everywhere. The white cotton blouse she was wearing became flecked with dots of ink.

I wanted to snatch the brush from her hands. Try to preserve at least a few of those precious markers. But all I could do was stand there, paralysed and mute, watching as she erased it all.

The last line to go was the one Dad had done, recording my height just two weeks previously. The one celebrating my tenth birthday.

1m 42 cms.

The wall was stained and patchy. There were places where she had eroded the whitewash, exposing ugly splodges of the pink mortar underneath.

'Better,' she said, when it was done.

That was the beginning. The beginning of a summer of family trauma which would end one Sunday morning with the slamming of a door and the sound of my mother's footsteps crossing the gravel of the drive. I raced out of bed and pressed my face against the glass of the window, just in time to see her climb into a taxi.

Later Dad found out she had withdrawn her savings and bought a narrowboat in which she could be truly alone.

Dad was sure she would come back, sure that her mind would readjust with time. But she didn't, and my world changed from that point.

I withdrew from my classmates. Pulling back from the small

rituals that bond children together. Party invitations went unanswered. Sleepovers were turned down.

'Better you don't lose your friends,' Dad told me kindly.

But I did lose them. And, I realise now, that by turning inwards, I lost a lot more as well. The yearning to laugh and run and play, to gossip and fall out and shift alliances on a whim and wonder together at the craziness of the adult world ... share life by growing together.

All of that was missing.

Instead I focused on becoming the person my Dad would most admire. And, deep down, I think I was trying to make sure that he too would not leave me. I focused on my studies, racing through the syllabus at breakneck speed. Finally, at the end of year eight, when it was clear the school I was at could no longer offer me what I needed, I left to be taught by tutors at home with help two days a week from Dad.

There was a price. I had to promise to see a therapist every month.

'It will help you, Becks,' Dad said.

'I'm fine, really,' I protested.

I knew I wasn't.

His name was Dr Manning, a psychiatrist friend of my father, based in a leafy south London suburb. He was a startlingly tall and skinny man, a full head higher than anyone I had ever met. He had shoulder-length hair and dressed like a hippy, his body folded into his chair like a stick insect striking a yoga pose.

I liked the renegade way his mind worked and sensed the feeling was mutual.

On the wall of his waiting room was a diploma from the Royal College of Psychiatrists. Our first conversation began with me asking him about the four butterflies that were included in the college coat of arms.

'Psyche was the ancient Greek word for life force or spirit and it is often represented by a butterfly,' he told me. 'It symbolises change and transformation.'

So the term 'psychiatry' means 'a healing of the soul or spirit'. I found the concept fascinating and felt differently about butterflies from that point of my life. Loved them, to be exact, for the things they teach us about patience and adaptation and the ways the future inevitably shapes us.

Then we talked. And it felt good.

'You really get this stuff, don't you?' Dr Manning told me with a curious frown at the end of the first session. I think he had never had a patient quite like me.

He was right though. I did get it.

Mum's decision to abandon us, and her inability to show me the least scrap of love in her new guise, had caused me to become ... a chrysalis. Emotionally dormant in every way, except in my love for my father and my desire to follow in his footsteps.

'You need to become a butterfly,' Dr Manning told me this year.

'Get out more, you mean?' I replied. We shared a smile.

But I knew the flaw in his proposal. The butterfly cannot *decide* when it will emerge, be free to fly. Those decisions are made by other powers, powers that are vast and obscure.

The pupa is trapped in the chrysalis until the world is ready for it to become a butterfly. And that is exactly how I felt.

I was waiting. But I had no idea what I was waiting for.

Monday. Back at the wall and there's only one thing on my mind: get that notebook back for Becca.

I scrub for a while and come up with this idea. I pick up my mobile and call this lad called Fraser who's old enough to have a motorbike. Well, he's old enough to have nicked one. 'I need your Honda,' I tell him.

'It's £5 an hour. Plus fuel.'

And I know it's a risk. Because that Honda hasn't got tax or insurance or anything. But what I'm planning is to wait until the Dog Poisoner heads off on that BMW of his at the end of the day. And I'm going to follow him. And get Becca's notebook back. One way or the other.

Fraser says he'll bring the Honda down later and I get back to scrubbing. Then I look over the wall and see something really surprising: Becca's dad is awake! He's out of the coma.

I get a good feeling when I see this; I know how pleased Becca will be.

He still looks groggy but he's talking at least – to the doctor with the blond hair. The chat doesn't look too friendly, then two other guys come in. Becca's dad is pushing them away. Then they inject him and the whole thing looks well stressy. It's a bit disturbing to be honest.

Afternoon creeps round. Becca and her driver arrive for their daily visit. And I've *got* to say something to her, so, when she walks past I say,

'Glad your dad's getting better.'

We're walking towards the hospital entrance. And the media scrum is as distracting as ever. Then Joe's words finally penetrate my brain:

'*Glad your dad's getting better.*'

I ponder on it. Why on earth would he say that? Then I remember that he's been spying over the top of the wall and I get this strange feeling.

'Liz. Hang on a minute. I just want to check something out.'

She pauses, with a mild tut of annoyance. I walk back the handful of steps. Luckily the photographers have got what they want so they leave me alone.

'What did you mean by that?' I ask him.

Joe stops his work and flashes me a look. I get it again. That weird little lightning bolt in my midriff. What is it about this boy?

'Just what I said,' he replies. 'Glad he's back talking and all that.'

'*Talking?* He's in a coma. He *can't* talk.'

He shrugs and says, 'Whatever.'

I can't work this out. For some reason I instinctively trust this boy Joe, but at the same time, what he's saying doesn't sound possible. Still, I have to give him a chance.

'All right. I know you've been spying over the top of the wall. I saw you. So what have you seen?'

'I saw him chatting with that doctor,' I tell her. 'The one with the blond hair. But your dad didn't look very happy. It almost looked like an argument.'

'My dad was upset?' she says.

'Yeah. He was trying to push the doctor away. Then these other two guys came in and held him down and they injected him.'

All the colour runs out of Becca's face.

'Other doctors held him down to *inject* him? Why on earth would they do that?'

She looks so pale and confused. And I want to tell her about Shammy, and the fact that I took the notebook and that the huge guy off the BMW has got it now. I want to be honest with her – try and sort this whole mess out, but I can't because just then the driver is there. She's been listening in on the conversation.

'This is a load of hot air,' she says. 'Let's get inside.' She pulls Becca away.

At that moment Derek arrives in his van. I spin him a story about how I've got to do something with my dad and he takes the ladder and cleaning stuff away and leaves me on my own.

I go over to the park. I have to wait for Fraser to turn up with the Honda.

Just have to hope the Dog Poisoner doesn't leave early today.

I sit by Dad's side. And he is still in the coma.

My brain is tripping on what Joe has told me. Dad talking? Just a short time ago? It's too bizarre to take seriously.

Even the consultant neurologist has told me to my face – in the corridor just now – that he cannot find a single sign of conscious brain activity.

It's utterly confusing. But somehow I have faith in Joe.

I've been in the room for about half an hour when I hear the ping of an incoming text. The duty nurse pulls out her mobile and reads it, a cloud of anger passing rapidly over her face.

'I'll be back in a minute. Just got something to sort out,' she says. 'You'll be all right here with him for a second won't you?'

'Sure. No problem.'

The nurse retreats to the corridor and starts a blazing row with someone (lover, husband, son?).

So I am on my own with Dad for the first time since the incident.

My eyes are drawn to the drip that he is being intravenously fed with. It occurs to me that I should know what this drug is, particularly after what Joe has just told me.

I take a good look at the sticker on the label of the drip. The label says:

SALINE SOLUTION

It makes sense. They are keeping him hydrated. But that's when I notice something a bit odd: the sachet of drug solution which is feeding into Dad's arm has been tampered with. It's curious – I can see straight away that a sticker has been placed over the plastic.

It *looks* official, authentic. But what information is hidden underneath it?

Gently, so I don't rip the sticker and give away my actions, I peel it back. I'm listening out for the footsteps of the duty nurse in the corridor and I'm horribly aware of the risk of getting caught in the act.

I have to get my thumbnail under the edge and slowly, painfully slowly, ease the sticker back. Gradually it comes, revealing the name of another drug underneath:

PENTOBARBITONE

I pull my iPad out of my bag and go online. I enter the name of the drug in the Google search box and watch an array of definitions and links come up.

And what I find is more shocking than I could possibly have imagined.

Pentobarbitone, it turns out, is a powerful barbiturate used to induce coma.

Induce coma.

Not ease a patient out of a coma, as the neurologist told me. *Induce* it. The revelation leaves me feeling brutally sick.

I click from one website to another. Surely there is a mistake? Is this just my paranoid state of mind jumping to conclusions? Then I get a further thought: the scans of the head injury. Are they false as well?

I cross to the lightbox, and quickly slip the plastic scan sheet from its envelope. Immediately I see there is a blank sticker in the bottom right hand corner. I peel it back and find the following name:

PETER RONALD CRANE

The whole room sways as I get an attack of vertigo. It's someone else's scan. The brain swelling belonged to this other person, whoever he is. Dad's head injury is bad, but not as bad as they are telling the world.

Everything I have been told here in this hospital is a *lie*.

It is a moment of absolute clarity. I now know exactly where I stand. I can trust no one.

I hear footsteps in the corridor. I quickly place the scan back in its sleeve and regain my seat just as the nurse comes back in.

'You all right, love?' she says. 'You look a bit pale.'

'Yes, thank you, just a bit dizzy, I think it might be a cold coming on,' I tell her.

I realise that Joe was telling the truth about seeing Dad talking. If they can induce a coma so effortlessly, then they can undoubtedly bring my dad out of it for a discussion. Or, it suddenly occurs to me, should the word be *interrogation*?

The temptation is there to reach forward and rip that sachet of barbiturate right off the stand. But I know I have to resist. For the moment I have to swallow my anger. If I reveal what I know then everything about this game will instantly change. And I get the feeling *that* could be extremely dangerous.

Little beads of sweat run down my back. My face flushes red as the nurse stares at me.

'I think you should leave,' she says. 'You really don't look well.'

Liz comes to the room and we walk the corridors towards the exit. I'm feeling nauseous. The pentobarbitone discovery has taken me to a really dark place.

'Are you OK?' Liz asks. I can feel her eyes boring into me. 'We can chat if you like.'

She's perceptive, my government minder. She's realised that something has happened.

'I'm just tired,' I tell her. A nagging pulse of pain starts up in my head.

What are my options now? What can I do? And who on earth can I trust?

PART 6

THE COOK ZONE

Patrick Eden: I've reached a prep room. This is where they've been cooking the viruses.

Police Command: You're breaking up. The signal's getting weak.

Patrick Eden: According to this chart the monkeys were infected today, just a few hours ago. This virus has been supercharged in some extraordinary way. What have they done to it?

Audio transcript from helmet mic worn by Patrick Eden, UK Government bioweapons inspector following emergency call at SYMBARON lab, Hampshire.

That joker Fraser turns up with the Honda. He parks it under the trees and I pay him twenty quid.

He leaves me his helmet and he jogs off across the park and I know those twenty notes will be going up in smoke as fast as he can roll up the reefers.

The motorbike's a bit of a mess. The side's all dented and the front headlight's cracked. All the more reason to get some unwelcome attention from the police.

If I'd sussed it earlier I would have asked him for a discount.

I check out the situation over at the hospital entrance. The Dog Poisoner is still in view. He's standing with the other press guys waiting for Becca to come out.

Patience. I press back into the shadows under the trees. Just got to wait for him to hit the road. Follow him to wherever he's going and take it from there.

I know it's going to be risky, but I must get that notebook back for Becca.

'There she is!' a cry goes up and the press pack is back at work. Becca and that driver of hers have walked out of the gateway and got mobbed again.

'Can you give us an update on your father, Rebecca?'

'Rebecca look this way! This way!'

I feel good about my secret knowledge. What would these guys give to have seen what I saw? Becca's dad awake and chatting. One photo of that would be front page all over the world within hours.

'Rebecca! Just a short statement! That's all we want.'

'She's got no comment,' Liz snaps.

A crazy urge bubbles up inside me.

'Rebecca! Look into the camera here. Just one pic!'

I could tell them. Tell them right now. Stand my ground and tell the truth about what I found out.

What a sensation that would cause. A crazy part of me wants to do it. But the rational side of me sees the reasons I must wait a little bit longer.

I must have proof. Photographic evidence of the pentobarbitone drip and the false scan. There was no time to get it just now with the nurse coming back in. But tomorrow I can try to find a way.

'Give us some breathing space will you?' Liz yells. She pushes back against the photographers as we approach the car.

If I do it without photos it will be my word against the entire might of the British government. My word against theirs. How will they paint me? A stressed out teenager who is angry and confused? A mentally disturbed girl who is seeing a psychiatrist? I've seen how they distorted the picture of Dad.

Camera flashes blitz us as we push forward. One of the photographers is jostled against a parked motorbike. The bike falls with a metallic crunch against the front of Liz's car.

There's this horrible crash. Becca's driver is shouting blue murder.

I wander over to see what's happening. The press guys are milling around in a state of high excitement.

A big Suzuki bike is being hauled away from that beautiful shiny Lexus. I push through and see the bike has dented the whole of the wing. There's a series of ugly scratches in the metal.

'This car is government property,' Becca's driver is ranting. She's getting right in the face of the bike owner.

I look towards Becca. She's standing on her own near the back of the car. I'd reckoned she'd be happier now her dad's out of the coma, but in fact she's looking even more gutted than before.

She seems a bit panicky as I walk towards her. But I need to tell her the truth.

'I found your notebook,' I blurt out. 'And I kept it.'

'What?' A scowl crosses Becca's face.

'I wanted to keep it safe for you. Stop the driver from getting it.'

'I've been worried sick,' she says. 'I thought it was lost for good.'

'Right. Sorry.'

'Have you got it with you?'

'Not exactly.'

This sticky silence kicks off between us.

The question hangs. Joe says nothing.

'Are you going to answer? Can I have the notebook back please?'

Joe gets this bright red blush in his cheeks.

'Erm, that might be a bit of a problem,' he says. 'Actually it's been stolen.'

'*Stolen*?' Anger uncoils inside me. 'You took my dad's notebook to keep it safe and then were stupid enough to let someone else steal it from *you*?'

'Yeah. And they killed my dog to get it.'

I take a deep breath. Joe's story is going a little too fast for my brain.

'What? Killed your *dog*? Why would they do that? I don't get it ... '

'It's that guy over there,' he continues in a whisper, pointing covertly to one of the photographers. 'The big one in the mirrored shades. He saw me pick up the notebook. He even got it on film. He stole my keys from my bag and must have followed me home.'

I stare at the photographer. Joe's story is sending me into a cold sweat.

'Who is he, Joe?' I whisper. 'What does he want?'

'No idea. But he came to our house when we were out. He put some poison through the front door and my dog must have eaten it.'

'That's evil.'

'Yeah. That was Shammy he killed. My Shammy.'

Becca pulls out a tissue. Her cheeks suddenly get shiny and slick with tears. In that moment I want to do something I've never wanted to do with any girl ever. I want to hold her. Make it better with a hug.

'Joe,' she says, 'I'm sorry about your dog, but this is a disaster for me too. That book might be dangerous. More dangerous than you can imagine.'

Suddenly I see the Dog Poisoner. It looks like he's packing up for the day. He puts his camera gear in the pannier of the BMW.

'The Dog Poisoner's leaving,' I tell her. 'I'm going to follow him.'

I'm holding my helmet. I slip it on to my head and clip the chinstrap.

'You can come with me if you like. There's a spare helmet on the back of the bike.'

Becca's eyes flash wide. Just for the tiniest moment.

'I can't do that.' Becca fixes a look to the front of the car. The driver's still busy trying to sort out the mess.

'I need to take your insurance details,' we hear her saying. The photographer opens up the topbox on his Suzuki, pulling out some paperwork.

'Don't trust my driving?' I ask her.

Becca half smiles.

'It's not that. I'll get into trouble with my minder,' she says.

'Whatever, I'll go on my own.'

I turn my back on Becca and head towards the bike.

Joe jogs away. He's heading for a motorbike parked up across the road.

That big photographer – what did Joe call him, the Dog Poisoner? – is pulling on his leather bike jacket.

My heart is pounding at some ferocious tempo. Joe reaches the bike. He's climbing on to it.

I can't break free from Liz. Can I? She'll be totally livid with me.

The giant pulls on his gloves. No one is paying any attention to me. For once.

A zillion things zap through my mind. Is the man who stole Dad's notebook connected to Benson and the government? Or is he connected to the secret lab where Hazelgrove was killed?

I sneak another look to Liz. She's utterly preoccupied. Joe's engine rips into life. He pulls out of the park.

Then something snaps inside me. I need to get Dad's notebook back at any cost.

Why should I play by the rules? No one else is. I pull a scrap of paper from my bag and scribble a note to Liz to tell her I need some space for a few hours and not to worry.

The Dog Poisoner roars off down the road. I run to Joe. I glance around. Liz has still not spotted my move away from the car.

'I'm coming with you,' I tell Joe. I pull on the spare helmet and jump on to the back of the bike. Half a second later we're ripping down the road and I'm clinging on to Joe for dear life.

And thinking: what the @&%! am I doing?

Underneath my helmet I'm grinning like a nutter.

Becca. On *my* bike! Well, a bike I've rented. Her hands around my waist. Her body pressed in tight against my back.

'I never thought you'd do this in a million years!' I shout back. 'I was more or less joking when I asked you if you wanted to come.'

'Don't talk!' she yells. 'Concentrate on following him!'

The Dog Poisoner pulls away fast, heading for west London. I keep a good distance behind, getting the measure of Fraser's bike.

I'm well nervous. Part of me thinks of what this big monster of a guy might do if he susses we're following him. He could get nasty – violent even.

And part of me just wants to do the best for Becca. And Shammy.

But it's not so easy, because he's riding a 1200cc BMW which is a bit of a beast, and we're on this 500cc Honda with an oil leak and two squidgy tyres.

Near Hammersmith I lose him in heavy traffic. There's too many trucks about, blocking my view.

'There he is!' Becca shouts in my ear. 'He's gone left at the roundabout.'

It feels good to have her so close. Insanely good.

I twist the throttle, ask the engine for a few more revs.

We're back on his tail.

109 BECCA

The Dog Poisoner is still in sight. We're weaving from one lane to another.

'Hope he's not going too far,' Joe calls back. 'We've only got half a tank of fuel.'

The traffic is heavy. We're missing cars by inches. Cutting people up. The occasional horn is blasting off. I can feel the red heat of the exhaust radiating through the air close to my right thigh.

'Just thinking about your driver,' Joe yells. 'She's going to go ape when she finds out you've done a runner.'

'Too right,' I tell him.

It's true about Liz. My getaway act is going to wind her up completely and I know I'm in for a rough ride when I get back.

I even feel kind of guilty about letting her down. Then there's Benson. How is the big boss going to react when he finds out I've gone AWOL?

Will he punish me? Prevent me going to the hospital to see Dad? That would stop me getting the photographs of the pentobarbitone ...

'Look out you idiot!' Joe jerks the bike to the right as a car cuts across us.

I cling on hard, both hands wrapped around Joe's midriff. It feels crazy when I think I hardly know this boy. And he is some kind of criminal after all.

He could be taking me anywhere.

'Lean into the bends,' he says. 'You're throwing us off balance.'

Then again it feels right to be on this bike with him. There's too much at stake not to be following every lead.

The Dog Poisoner works his way out of London. It's more or less OK to follow him because there's so many red lights and the traffic is stop-start. We get to Kingston upon Thames and there's a bad moment when we think we've lost him again.

But at the last second we see the BMW, driving up the ramp on to the A3.

Now he's riding like a madman, dodging in and out of the traffic. I follow him at a bit of a distance. He mustn't see us. Mustn't know we're on his tail.

'I'm freezing to death!' Becca yells after half an hour.

The ride goes on. We enter Surrey. He's going further than I thought. I can feel Becca shivering with the wind chill and I wish I had some gloves.

'My house is about twenty minutes away from here,' Becca shouts.

We're driving through countryside. Green fields on all sides. Now I'm getting really nervous I might run out of petrol.

He turns off the main road. Starts to ride through some lanes. I drop back even further.

Finally he stops at this massive gate. It looks like the entrance to some sort of palace and there's a sign next to it that says:
THE MISSION OF RECONCILIATION AND PEACE

The Dog Poisoner speaks briefly into an intercom. The gates swing open and he disappears inside. Two black Range Rovers with tinted windows follow him in from the road.

'A mission?' Becca says. 'That's pretty much the last thing I was expecting.'

111 BECCA

We stare at the entrance. Inside the gates we can see uniformed guards. A huge wall embraces the property, stretching right down the road. It looks like an old stately home, but with tighter security.

'This place gives me the creeps,' Joe says. 'It looks more like a prison.'

'Maybe we should move,' I suggest. 'There's a guard staring at us.'

We ride around a corner and find some woods where we can stop. Joe kills the engine and we hide the bike in some bushes.

'What do you say we pop over the wall and take a look inside?' Joe asks.

'What if there's dogs? Those guards looked pretty mean.'

Joe smiles. 'I'll go. Don't want you to slip out of your comfort zone.'

My stomach churns. I bite my lip, not wanting Joe to sense my fear.

'OK,' I tell him. 'Let's go.'

We run across the road. The wall looks ridiculously high now we're standing at the foot of it.

'Give me a leg up,' Joe says. I hold out my hands.

Joe steps in. He jumps. Gets a grip and scrambles to the top. Suddenly I hear a car coming.

'Quick!' Joe holds his arms down. I jump and grab his wrists.

He hauls me up in a single powerful move. We're on the top of the wall. Trees are hiding us.

Joe sees the alarm straight away. 'Breaker beam,' he says. 'Sophisticated stuff.'

Becca is staring at the alarm. I have to smile at the stressy look on her face.

'Looks like this is as far as we'll get,' she says.

'There's always a weak spot,' I tell her.

'How do you know?'

'The graffiti spraying. Dodging alarms is a part of the game.'

Within a few seconds I spot it. One of the trees is overhanging in a way that means we can swing over the laser beam.

I shuffle along the wall and take the jump. Fly for a second. Get my hands round the branch, swing up my legs. I scuff my way along to the end of the branch and drop down.

'You really think I can do that?' Becca hisses. Her face has gone white.

'Shhhh!' I wait a few seconds, ears alert.

No dogs. No distant shouts or sirens.

'OK. Go for it.'

She repeats my move along the wall, then freezes at the point of no return. Both her legs are shaking.

'Stop wasting time!'

She glares at me, then takes the jump. Does better than I thought. She drops down out of the tree, looking proud.

We're in.

113 BECCA

'What next?' I ask.

'There's some buildings over that way.'

We creep slowly through the forest. The floor is spongy with pine needles and the air is filled with the smell of resin. My whole body is on some insane level of alert.

A blackbird erupts from a bush. I nearly jump out of my skin. Gradually we see forms through the trees – the soaring towers and rooftops of a stately home.

'Wait!' Joe says.

He gestures to our right. There's a grey concrete bunker standing on its own, the type that was built during the Second World War.

'Let's check it out,' he says. We move stealthily across. As we get closer we see that the entrance to this crumbling old bunker has been fitted with shiny steel bars. We approach cautiously, tiptoeing up and staring into the gloomy interior.

'Something's moving in there,' Joe whispers.

In the darkest recesses of the bunker a shadow stirs. Joe and I flash a shocked look at each other. Then a figure emerges.

It's a girl with straggly dreadlocks. Twenty years old at a guess. She's dressed in a dirty black tracksuit and looks pale and undernourished. She locks eyes with me.

'You know Melzack will kill you if he finds you out and about without your black rags,' she says.

Becca examines the barred doorway. It's sealed with a hefty brass padlock.

'Who's locked you up like this?' she asks.

The girl scratches at her arm. Her fingernails are black with grunge.

'Melzack, of course.'

She looks us up and down with strangely dead eyes.

'Who?'

'Melzack. He's the boss. Who are you guys anyway? Cos I'll get another twenty-four hours in this dump if we're seen talking.'

'We sneaked in,' Becca says.

'You broke *in* here?' The girl starts to laugh, exposing yellow-stained teeth. 'That's a first!'

'So what did you do to piss off this Melzack guy?' I ask.

She leans in towards the bars and I see an ugly dark blue bruise on her neck.

'They caught me with a mobile phone,' she replies. 'One of the seven deadly sins.'

'You got slammed up for *that*?'

'The nights are the worst. You wouldn't believe what kind of creepy crawly stuff there is in a craphole like this. I'm talking earwigs, beetles, mosquitoes; it's impossible to sleep. Hey! You guys got some tobacco?'

'Sorry, no smokes,' Joe tells her. 'You OK for water and stuff?'

'There's a bottle of water and a packet of cream crackers to keep me alive,' she says. 'Oh, and there's a dirty old mattress and a bucket. But I'm never getting locked up in this bunker again, I can tell you.'

'When did you join this place?' I ask.

'Three years ago. Biggest mistake *ever*, signing up with Melzack.'

'Why don't you just climb over the wall and escape?'

'I tried to run away six months ago but they brought me back. I was beaten and held in a cell on my own for a week.'

'Can't you go to the police?'

The girl bites her lip.

'I've had trouble with the police. That's one of the reasons I ended up as one of Melzack's disciples in the first place. My parents chucked me out. I didn't get on in the hostels.'

She is clutching the bars hard. Her knuckles are white.

'There's something else,' the girl goes. 'My younger brother is here too and I'm frightened they'll take it out on him. He's still all starry eyed about Melzack and he won't listen to his big sister.'

A crashing noise shakes the trees nearby. The girl gasps, jumping into the shadows. 'It's just pigeons,' I tell her. She edges back into the light.

'How many people has Melzack recruited?' Becca asks.

'About a hundred and fifty. From all over the world. It's like the United Nations in here. Me and my bro are two of the only Brits.'

'How does he persuade them to join?' I ask. 'I mean, if he treats people as badly as he treats you?'

'Most of the people here are really young, not much more than kids really, recruited from war zones. That's where he has his missions, Chechnya, Sierra Leone, Iraq – anywhere that there's chaos and fighting. He picks the orphans, the ones that have lost everything, offers them a shiny new future in England.'

'Clever,' Becca says.

'Oh, he's clever all right is Mr Croak. A lot of them are boy soldiers, kids that are messed up. Scary kids. The type that can easily get radicalised. To them Melzack is a hero. They worship him, literally, and they'll do anything he asks.'

'Mr Croak?'

'That's his secret nickname. If you ever hear him you'll find out why.'

Becca reaches in her pocket and pulls out a scrap of paper and a pencil.

'Let me give you this.' She scribbles on the paper then passes it through the bars.

'My email. Let me know if there's a way we can help you. Also, if you hear anything about a stolen notebook, will you tell me?'

'OK. It's a deal. My name's Tanya by the way.'

117 BECCA

We leave the bunker and push through the pines, heading towards the building we can see through the trees.

'That was pretty scary,' Joe whispers.

'Yeah. If that's how this man Melzack treats his followers what do you think he can do to his enemies?'

I follow Joe, stepping carefully to minimise noise, and there's another question ticking away in my mind: what does this psycho want with Dad's notebook?

We walk for some minutes, then Joe parts the branches at the forest boundary.

'Looks like Buckingham Palace,' he says.

The mission grounds have opened up in front of us. Dominating everything is a mansion built from unattractive grey stone. Gargoyles gurn from the upper parapets. The roof has lost a few hundred slates. The masonry around the windows looks chipped and worn.

The house is surrounded by temporary huts with a military look to them. It feels like an army camp.

There's plenty of people moving from building to building, dressed in black tracksuits. There's even some uniformed security guards, patrolling about.

'Look!' I nudge Joe. 'Over there!'

It's the Dog Poisoner's motorbike, parked up at the side of the mansion.

'Let's move round,' Becca says.

We stick in the cover of the forest, doing a loop round the big house and ending up in some thick bushes not far from the bike.

Now I'm getting pumped. We're seriously close to the action. If we get spotted now there's no way we'll make it back to the wall. 'It's some kind of lab,' Becca says.

We can see people through the windows. The Dog Poisoner's in there, changed out of his bike gear. Five others – four men and one woman – are with him, sitting round a big table. Then this new bloke sweeps in and the others sit up and pay attention.

The new guy is kind of freaky looking. He's so thin he looks like he's starving. He has long, black, straggly hair and a weirdly pale face. He moves in a stiff, robotic way. His white tracksuit is hanging off him like it's far too big. There's something strange about his neck. I see a flash of metal there.

The others stop talking and I can see they are respectful of this new guy so I assume he has to be the leader or something.

'That must be Melzack,' Becca whispers. 'I need to hear what he's saying. If I can get across to those bins ... '

I see the two bins she's talking about – big industrial ones, right underneath the open window.

'I'm going for it,' Becca whispers. She sprints across the path and makes it to the bins. She gets away with the risky move. No one has spotted her.

And I'm thinking, well, this girl is either crazily brave or crazily crazy. Or possibly both.

PART 7
THE WET ROOM

Patrick Eden: I'm in the wet room. There's a dissection table here. A glass panel through to the main part of the lab.

Police Command: Can you see Hazelgrove?

Patrick Eden: Yes, I can see him now. He's crawling across the floor towards the glass. (Sounds of screaming.) He's bleeding – there's blood everywhere … everywhere.

Audio transcript from helmet mic worn by Patrick Eden, UK Government bioweapons inspector following emergency call at SYMBARON lab, Hampshire.

I wedge myself between the bins.

The bones in my head are shuddering with each beat of my heart. Adrenaline is running faster with every breath. At any second I'm expecting someone to lean out of the window and yell in my face.

Count to ten. Breathe slowly. Get myself back together.

I raise my head. There's a gap between the plastic bags of rubbish on top of the bins. I can see into the lab.

The man with the long, black hair takes his position at the top of the table. He picks up a small microphone and holds it close to his neck. I see a metal chain there and a small circular valve.

Now I understand. There's a hole directly into his larynx. A tracheotomy. He's had his voice box removed. He has to form words by forcing air out of the hole.

Mr Croak. Tanya's cruel nickname now makes sense.

'It's one week ... since the lab ... was raided ... and closed down,' he says.

His speech is punctuated by pauses. During each gap he takes a couple of seconds to swallow and grab a ragged breath. It sounds and looks painful. His deep black eyes are bulging with the effort.

'You know ... that ... Hazelgrove ... is dead.'

A middle-aged man with a moustache stands up. I guess he might be Arabic, about forty years old. His accent is strong, Middle Eastern.

'Dark Heart is in serious trouble, is it not? What guarantees can you give us that our investment will still pay off?'

Melzack smiles confidently.

'Everything is still ... under control ... We put a bug ... into

Hazelgrove's widow's house ... The government came and ... interrogated her but ... she had nothing ... to tell them. Then we got ... this.'

He clicks a handset and a video image appears on a screen. It's a fuzzy, clandestine shot of two people on a sofa. One is a woman I've never seen before in my life. She's clutching a hanky to her face. The other I recognise; it's Dad! It's all I can do to stop myself crying out.

The video plays. I crane my neck a bit more to hear it. The lady is angry, tears running down her cheeks. It looks like Dad is trying to console her. She pushes his hand away.

'What killed Simon? Why won't they tell me?' she sobs.

'I'll find out in the next few days,' Dad tells her. 'They took me off the case but I kept a sample of the virus and I'm going to analyse it as soon as I can.'

The video freezes. Melzack nods to the Dog Poisoner who picks up the story.

'As soon as we knew Eden had stolen a sample of the virus we decided to move. We brought the hit team in and raided his house at dawn two days ago. Things got a bit messy but we removed the sample from his secret lab, rigged up a suicide scenario to cover our tracks.'

Acid rises in my throat. I have to fight back the urge to be sick. Confirmation. It was Melzack's team that tried to murder Dad. And them that destroyed the Ice House.

The woman interrupts him. She is wearing tinted glasses and her red hair is pulled back into a tight knot. Her accent sounds like she may be from Russia.

'Is it the virus? It had better be. You won't find another scientist like Hazelgrove again.'

The room goes absolutely silent.

'Well?' she snaps.

Melzack makes a strange choking sound in his throat.

'It was labelled ... "Dark Heart",' he says, ' ... but we've now ... done the tests and ... '

'It's not the virus?' The woman spits the words.

'No,' the Dog Poisoner responds. 'It's an inert compound. Eden must have switched the label as a safety measure. He tricked us.'

'We *need* that sample,' another of the delegates insists urgently. He's Asian, but I can't tell exactly where he's from. He looks a little like the people in Dad's photos from conferences he attended in Kazakhstan or Uzbekistan.

'All of our investment is for nothing if we don't have it.'

'It has to be in Eden's vault,' the Dog Poisoner continues. 'But the place is teeming with police at the moment and it's protected by a code that only Eden knows.'

'Our best bet is ... to get Patrick Eden,' Melzack says. 'One way ... or another.'

'We've heard rumours about a notebook,' the Asian man continues. 'With notes about the vaccine. What's the deal with that?'

Melzack gestures for the Dog Poisoner to answer.

'We've been staking out the hospital where Eden is held,' the Dog Poisoner replies. 'And we saw an opportunity to get hold of a notebook his daughter was stupid enough to lose.'

I bite the inside of my lip, swamped with a rush of anger and guilt.

He reaches out for the handset. A few seconds later I see scribbles and writing come up on a video screen. He's projecting pages from Dad's notebook. The section titled 'Vaccine/ Hazelgrove'.

'You won't get enough recruits if you don't have the vaccine,' the woman says. 'Not everyone is prepared to give their life for the cause.'

'Correct ... ' Melzack agrees. 'We need just ... another ... twenty-four hours ... to figure ... these notes out ... and recreate it.'

'Now ... ' the Arab raises a hand. 'How about the schools? How many have you identified?'

The schools? What schools?

'So far there ... are twenty-three,' Melzack says. 'All with strong ... connections to the military.'

He nods to the Dog Poisoner. A map of the UK gets screened, dotted at random points with red stars.

'Some are close to military establishments like Sandhurst,' Melzack's deputy continues. 'So they are filled with the sons and daughters of British army personnel. Others are right next to some of the fourteen American air bases in the UK, packed with American kids whose mothers and fathers are posted there.'

'Good,' another of the delegates responds. He looks Latin American. 'How will the virus be deployed?'

'We'll strike ten minutes before assembly times,' the Dog Poisoner continues. 'Just before the pupils are gathered together. Every school will be targeted by a separate member of our team and each operative will be protected by vaccination. They'll be posing as groundsmen, equipped with high-pressure backpack spraying devices. Once they are inside the school, two minutes of spraying will fill the hall with odourless, invisible gas. The pupils will walk in and become infected immediately. The success rate will be close to 100 per cent.'

'The authorities ... will be overwhelmed ... ' Melzack says. 'There are only ... about 200 ... isolation units in British hospitals ... but we will be ... creating 20,000 victims ... they will have to ... lockdown the schools ... seal them off ... while the children ... die.'

My fists curl, the nails digging deep into my palms. My leg is cramping up. As I shift it I make a small noise on the gravel.

The Dog Poisoner spins round, stares in my direction. I duck, my heart ripping wildly. It's time to get out of this crazy place. All thoughts of getting the notebook back are now lost. After what I've seen and heard, Joe and I will be lucky to get out at all.

I dodge back across the lawn and make it to the cover of the bushes where Joe is waiting for me.

'What are they saying?' he asks.

'I'll tell you later. We need to get out of here.'

I glance back. I can see the Dog Poisoner looking out of the window. Did he see me? I can't tell.

Joe leads the way. Sprinting through the trees. At any moment I expect to hear dogs on our trail or the pounding of feet on the forest floor.

Suddenly Joe stops. He looks confused.

'There's a building ahead,' he whispers. 'There might be guards inside.'

'You're not lost are you?'

'Give me one second, that's all.'

I flash a look over my shoulder.

'Joe! Leave it. We have to get to the wall!'

Joe sneaks closer to investigate. Then he beckons me forward and I stare through a crack in the door to see two bright yellow cars.

'Toyota GT86s,' Joe whispers. 'Monster vehicles! They're the type of motors that getaway drivers use for bank jobs.'

'Whatever! Let's keep moving,' I tell him.

Three minutes later we're back at the wall.

'I'll go first,' Joe says.

He jumps for the branch. Swings up and over, then reaches down and helps me up.

We drop down on to the verge and dash across the lane.

Joe drags the motorbike out of the bushes. I jam on my helmet and check my mobile. Thirteen messages from Liz. I've been gone for three hours.

The engine rips into life and we hit the road at reckless speed. I grab on to Joe even harder than before, terrified of falling off. As we ride past the entrance we see the Dog Poisoner run up to the iron gates. He watches us. Then turns back.

'Hope he doesn't follow us on his bike!' Joe shouts back.

We rip down the lane, leaning into the corners as the world blurs past. Then Joe stiffens.

'I can see him following in the mirror,' Joe says fearfully. 'He's about a mile behind, but he's going to catch us. We're heavier, slower.'

We keep going. I'm hoping for a turning off the road but there are none. Then I see a train trundling across the countryside miles off to our right.

A sign flashes past. We're approaching a town. I remember seeing the station on the outskirts.

'Joe! You'll be faster without me. Drop me at this station. I'll get a train to London.'

Joe pulls into the station forecourt and I jump off the back of the bike.

We lock eyes for a long moment.

'Epic,' he says.

'You could say that.'

'See you at the hospital tomorrow?'

'Yes.'

He revs the bike and pulls away, leaving me in a smoky blue cloud of petrol fumes.

'Hey, thank you!' I call after him. But I don't know if he hears me.

I rush to the platform just as the London train is pulling in. No time for a ticket. I jump on board and the doors close tight behind me with a hiss of air.

As the train lurches into life I see the motorbike coming very fast down the road from the direction of Melzack's mission.

Joe has a race on his hands.

120 JOE

I rip the throttle wide open. Speeding through the town.

In my mirror, the BMW. Closing in fast.

Seventy miles per hour. Eighty. I beg every last scrap of speed out of this old beast as I hit countryside again.

A lay-by ahead. A cop car is lurking there. First time in my life I've been grateful to see them! Getting busted is going to be bad news but better than what the Dog Poisoner has planned for me.

I flash them the finger as I speed past.

Twenty seconds later it's the siren and flashing blue lights.

I swerve on to the verge and stop the engine. The cops park up behind me.

The Dog Poisoner drives slowly past, staring me out furiously as he goes.

The cops check me out. Then they check out the bike.

'Let me see,' one of the cops says as he scans his notebook. 'You're underage. No licence. Never passed a test. No insurance. No road tax. Your bike is stolen and has illegal lights, illegal tyres, illegal indicators and dodgy brakes.'

'They're going to throw the book at you, sonny Jim,' another tells me.

And I know he's right. Books will definitely be thrown. Let alone what my Dad's going to do. I *know* he's going to go ape on this one. After the promises I've made him and all.

It makes my head ache all over just thinking about it.

The train winds a leisurely route, trundling without urgency towards London. My mind, by contrast, is racing at maximum velocity as I try to catch up with the revelations of the day.

It was Melzack's team that tried to kill Dad.

Now they are preparing some atrocity involving a deadly virus. There are schools involved.

What can I do? Who can I tell? I have to *act*. Have to do something fast. The police. I should just go straight to the police.

I take out my mobile. I swipe it open and I'm about to dial 999. Then I reconsider.

If I go to the police, who is to say they won't just hand me straight to Benson? And, if I reveal what I know about Melzack, what proof can I offer? None. I can't prove a thing. There was a conversation, overheard by me and me alone. And even if the police raided Melzack's place what would they find? Melzack hasn't got the deadly virus; that was clear from the meeting.

So much is at stake. I have to take the right path through this maze.

Then there's the government angle. Defence HQ's desperation to shut Dad up. Drug him into silence. Prevent him telling the truth about Melzack's secret lab. I can't prove that either. The slightest wrong move by me could tip the scales. Kick the hornets' nest and mess everything up for good.

Deep down I fear that Dad's life may still be in the balance.

My mobile pings to announce an incoming email. My hand is shaking as I click it open.

122 JOE

They chuck me in the back of the cop car. And all the way back to London what we saw at that mission place is whizzing round my head. That girl Tanya, locked up in the stinking bunker. The members dressed in black. The sinister meeting that Becca listened in on. What does it all mean?

Also I think about Becca. Is she OK? Did she get a train? What clues did she hear when she sneaked up to the window? What does that man Melzack want with her dad's notebook? It makes me feel sick just to think about it.

I have to tell Dad what I've seen. Need to get his advice about what to do, before it's too late.

The cops take me to the police station nearest my house and they call Dad in. When he joins me in the detention room his face is like a blank mask. He nods when they say we have to wait for a social worker to arrive, but he still doesn't say a single word to me.

'Dad, something happened today,' I tell him. 'There's a reason I got busted on the bike. I wasn't doing anything bad, I promise.'

He holds up his hand to shut me up. His eyes are different, colder than ever before.

I try again but he just picks up a newspaper and starts to read. I don't know what he's thinking. I don't know what he's going to do.

It's terrifying.

123 BECCA

I check out the message:

Hi Rebecca. Hope you don't mind me getting in touch.
My name is Cora, I'm Simon Hazelgrove's daughter.

Cora. I remember Dad mentioning her just before the melt-down incident when he smashed the greenhouse.

I've been trying to find out more about how my dad
died and I suddenly thought maybe we should meet up.
I've discovered some things which make me think your
dad was right; that the government is hiding the truth.
I'm thinking of talking to a journalist about it but I thought
I'd try to speak to you first. Maybe you can help me?

I think about Cora's situation, feeling a strong sense of empathy for her. The two of us are in similar situations, both trying to discover the reality behind a cloak of lies.

I think about her idea. Is she right? Is talking to a journalist the way to go?

It's an intoxicating thought. No way they could harm Dad once the truth was out. And it would put Melzack on the run. My gut reaction is **yes**, **yes**, **yes!** Let's blow their lies and deceit wide open for the world to see.

I need to get Dad home. Where he belongs.

Then, with crushing suddenness, the reality of the situation swamps me. What will happen? How will the government react? Can they stop a newspaper from publishing if it is a matter of national security? Will Cora and I be seen as whistle-blowers just like Dad? Might we even end up in some prison somewhere?

I decide to take a risk on it. There's not a second to lose. I dial the mobile number at the bottom of Cora's email.

'Cora? It's Rebecca Eden.'

We start hesitantly, and I can hear the catch of emotion in her voice. She tells me how sorry she is about Dad's 'suicide' attempt, adding that she doesn't believe he would ever have done it.

'I've hardly slept since my dad died,' she tells me. 'And Mum's all over the place. We're trying to work out what really happened, but now your dad's in a coma there's no one to help us.'

I feel a surge of compassion for her. My situation seems desperate but at least I have the *hope* I will get my Dad back.

Then she says: 'Rebecca, shall we meet? I'm in London now, if you can make it.'

My mind flicks through a few possibilities.

'How about the cafe at the British Library?' I ask her.

'Perfect. I could be there at four.'

'OK. I'm on my way.'

One hour later I am putting my bag through the security scanners and entering the soaring atrium of the British Library. It's now five hours since I ran away from Liz and I can only imagine how hostile things are going to be when I get back. Luckily, Cora turns up at the same moment.

I check her out as she walks over, resetting my mind from the erroneous assumptions I'd made about how she'd look. I'd imagined a bookish girl, dressed perhaps in a plaid skirt and cashmere cardigan.

In fact she's more the type of girl you might see browsing the stalls at Camden Market, dressed in skinny black jeans and a denim jacket. On her feet she wears a scuffed pair of Timberlands. Her hair is long and dark, her face extremely pale, almost porcelain white.

She seems to be a goth, but not because of make-up. Her natural look has the goth effect.

'Hi,' she says. 'I recognised you from the newspaper pictures.'

She gives me a stiff hug. When she pulls back she tries to smile. The effort twists her mouth into an oddly stiff expression. There's something strange about the way the muscles move in her face, like she's been partly paralysed.

'How long do you think we've got?' she asks.

'Twenty minutes?' I suggest. 'I'm on the run from my minder so I can't spend long.'

'OK.'

We grab two teas and sit at a table in a quiet corner of the cafe. And I'm bursting to tell her about the pentobarbitone and everything that happened at Melzack's mission. But I warn myself to be cautious. I have to be sure about her first. Got to know if I can trust her with this most sacred of secrets.

'How do you want to start?' I ask.

'I need to know why my dad is dead,' she says bitterly. 'And why the government is covering it all up.'

'Are they still blaming it on a gas explosion?'

'Yeah. They won't even admit there's been an autopsy. They say Dad was cremated in the fire.'

Her eyes well up. She pulls a tissue from a pack.

'You know he was working on bioweapons, right?'

'Sure, but he never told us much,' Cora says, shaking her head. 'He seemed pretty paranoid about everything.'

'That's not surprising. My dad's the same. And that was *before* he became a whistle-blower.'

'Your dad's the only person telling the truth in all of this,' she continues. 'The rest of them are lying through their teeth.'

'Have they stripped your house?' I ask.

'Yeah. Computers, tablets, notebooks, the works.'

'They gave me a minder,' I tell her. 'I can't blow my nose without Dad's ex-boss knowing about it.'

She nods sympathetically, then pulls a sheet from her bag.

The paper is covered with the symbols. The symbols of the Behenian Fixed Stars that guard the door to the Ice House.

I feel the skin on my arms prickle. A strange chill runs through me.

'Do you know what these are?' Cora asks casually. 'Your dad left it at our house by mistake. I thought I'd better keep it safe.'

'He left these at your house?' My mind churns with questions. Why would my father make such a silly mistake?

'Yeah. I'm guessing they're some sort of code aren't they?'

Cora stares at me. The warmth in her ebony eyes has dimmed just a fraction.

'I don't know,' I tell her. I don't want to get sidetracked into this now. There are more important things to discuss and the clock is ticking.

'I'm really interested to know what they are,' she persists. 'We could try and solve them together.'

'Really, I have no idea,' I say. 'Besides, there are other things I need to tell you about.'

Now is the moment. And I know that the way this goes will completely re-shuffle the pack. It's like stepping over the edge of a very high cliff, knowing you have no parachute.

'Cora, there are two questions I need to ask you: have you heard of a man called Melzack? And do you know anything about a drug called pentobarbitone?'

Five minutes later. Cora is up to speed. The false information on the drip. The fact that Joe saw my father being interrogated when he was supposed to be unconscious. Her father's role working for Melzack. The theft of Dad's notebook and the raid on our house. The atrocity Melzack is planning.

The school connection. Everything.

It just all comes out in a great rush of words and emotion. And it feels so good so tell someone – almost like a confession.

At first Cora is writing notes. Now she has stopped.

'They're evil,' she says quietly. 'All of them.'

Now it's me that has the tears kicking in. Cora plucks a tissue out of the pack and hands it across the table.

'There's a journalist that's been emailing me,' she says. 'Why don't we talk to him together? As soon as we can.'

'Sure,' I say. 'It makes sense. But we have to get proof of what they're doing. I need to get photographs of the pentobarbitone drip. And we need to find out more about Melzack.'

'OK,' she agrees. 'So let's split the jobs. You get the proof about what's happening to your dad. I'll do some research into Melzack. There's bound to be stuff I can find online.'

Her words fill me with confidence. This route feels right. If I can get the proof, and Cora finds out more about Melzack, we can talk to the journalist tomorrow. And maybe, in the end, justice will be done.

My mobile vibrates to signal an incoming text. It's from Liz, her seventeenth message of the day.

Where are you? Call me immediately.

I show the screen to Cora. She puts her hand on mine. At this moment, the warmth of that human contact is everything I need.

'It's great we can team up on this,' she says. 'I think we're making the right move.'

'Yes. This time tomorrow we'll get our chance to tell the truth.'

I try to sound confident but in my belly I am playing host to this tumour of fear.

124 JOE

The social worker turns up after an hour. She reads the police reports for a bit then fixes me with this nasty look.

'It depends on the judge, Joe,' she says. 'But sometimes they go for shock tactics in the case of a persistent offender like you. They might push for a custodial sentence.'

Then the room really does go quiet.

'Where would they send him?' goes my Dad.

'In this case it would probably be Feltham.'

And Dad glares at me. 'Well. If that's what the judge decides I'll back him all the way.'

And that's when my heart breaks into a thousand little bits. Dad's ready to chuck me out. Have me locked away in Feltham Young Offenders.

And I just get this deepest ever ache inside. Like I've been poisoned. Or flooded out with something evil. And it's almost as bad as when he told me that Mum had died.

'Dad ... ?' I'm so choked up I can hardly get a word out.

'I've already given you your last chance,' he says.

'But ... '

'I'm not interested in any excuses, Joe,' he says. 'You've done what you've done and that's the end of it.'

'We'll let you know when the date is set for the court case,' a policeman says.

'You can make your own way home,' Dad says. And then he's gone.

I walk out of the police station. And there's no way I'm going home. The way things have just gone I'm not even sure I've still got one.

There's rain in the air. It's not exactly cold but I feel this icy sensation inside. I head towards the shops. I'm thinking about

Becca and wondering how I can get in touch with her.

Then what happens is this: that nutter Fraser comes out of an alley with two dirty-looking mates and his face lights up when he sees me.

'I been looking for you,' he says. 'Where's my bastard bike?'

Fraser's two meatheads grab me by the scruff of the neck. And they march me off towards the estate.

I know I'm in for a bit of aggro. But, to be honest, compared with the other stuff in my life right now, it's no big deal. I can deal with violence. It's the rejection I can't handle.

We get to the back of the estate. There's a dusty scrap of waste ground there and Fraser plops himself down on this manky old sofa like he's the king of England, with me sitting on my arse in the dirt.

'Right,' he goes. 'What's happened to my bike?'

He lights up a spliff and blows smoke right in my face.

'The cops have got it.'

I'll tell you what it is about someone smacking you in the face with their fist. And this is something that only a person who has *been* smacked in the face could ever tell you: it makes you realise how the whole of your head is just one great big chunk of bone. Because there's no padding, or softness about it. It's just really *really* surprisingly *hard*. And your brain sort of goes **zap** with the impact of it.

Straight away I can taste blood. And his two mates are glittering with the sight of it; they're like attack dogs waiting for the order to get savage.

'I want £120 a day. Or you can get me a brand new Honda if you like. I'll settle for that.'

'Whatever.'

One of his mates kicks me well hard in the arse as I go.

I start to walk towards home. Rain is coming now, heavy

and fast. I'm still bleeding from my mouth and I'm wondering how I can sort things out with my dad.

And I think a good thought: at least things can't get any worse. They can only get better from now on.

Then my mobile's buzzing in my pocket. I check the screen. *It's Pauline.*

Her voice is thick with tears and she blurts it right out:

'They've got your dad. The police are at the yard now.'

I cut the call. I start to run.

I race through the streets. It's raining more. I'm soaked to the skin but I hardly care. And I'm sprinting faster than I've ever done before.

Don't let it be true. Please don't let it.

Then I'm there, running into the yard. And it is true. There's police cars there. Dogs. Customs and Excise people going through Dad's papers. Pauline's crying her eyes out in his office.

And in the middle of it, I see my dad. Looking pale and shaky.

'Someone tipped them off,' he tells me. There's two lines of tears running down his cheeks. 'It's over, Joe. It's all over.'

Then they're taking him away. And I'm chasing after the policeman, my fists balled up with the stress of the moment. 'What's going to happen? What's going to happen now?'

'Your dad's coming down to the station and he'll be questioned.'

'Then you'll let him home, right?'

The cop gives me a really nasty look. 'I don't think he's coming home for a bit,' he says.

They snap a pair of handcuffs on my dad. He's bright red with the shame of it. Then they chuck him in the back of a van and drive away.

At that moment I see someone on a BMW motorbike, sitting in the shadows way down the street. He drives away fast when he sees me clock him. But I know exactly who it is.

I smack my fist as hard as I can into the side of Dad's Transit. It leaves this massive great dent and my hand hurts like crazy.

I do it again and again. Until my knuckles are bleeding.

I put in a call to Liz and ask her to meet me at the local station. I have to hold the handset at arm's length while she vents off a volcanic eruption of rage.

'I've been texting you all day!' she snaps as soon as I get into the car. 'You could have had the courtesy to reply.'

'I needed some time alone,' I tell her. 'My mind just hit over-load with all the journalists fighting and everything. I spent the day wandering round the Natural History Museum.'

'I had to tell Benson that you'd disappeared,' she spits. 'He was seriously pissed off with you. And seriously pissed off with me for losing track of you.'

I say nothing. My attitude is changing, hardening as each day passes.

I never asked for a minder; Liz was forced on me. I have the right to do my own thing.

'You mustn't vanish like that again,' she says. 'Benson will ground you if you do.'

Ground me? A prisoner in my own house. A cold sweat breaks out on my back. I never thought of that.

Liz shuts up and my mind turns to Joe. Did he get away from the Dog Poisoner? I wish I had a mobile or email for him; things happened so fast we never swapped numbers.

As we reach home a message pings into my phone. To my surprise it's Tanya from Melzack's mission. I go straight to my room to read it.

'Hey. They released me from the bunker today. You said you'd like to know more about Melzack so I got my brother to sneak me into the tech room so I could send you these docs. One is the biography he gives his most trusted people. The other is a copy of the video he shows all the new recruits.'

I open the document:

JON MELZACK

Jon Melzack is a mission leader and peace campaigner. Born in Toronto, the son of a Methodist preacher, Jon had a troubled childhood and became a member of the notorious 'Outlaws' biker gang. Convicted of drug trafficking at the age of nineteen he served three years in the toughest of Toronto's prisons. It was during his time in solitary confinement that Jon saw a vision which led him to renounce his violent past.

In 2010 Jon achieved a lifelong dream and set up a peace camp in northern Kenya, Africa, attracting disciples from all over the world. The focus was on 'resistance through prayer', a multicultural vision reflecting Jon's belief in the need for a new world order based on mutual respect and reconciliation.

After two years the mission was mistakenly identified as a terrorist training camp by the American military. A drone attack dropped six missiles. Dozens of Jon's disciples (including his wife) were killed. The Americans later justified the operation as 'anti-terrorist' on the basis that shotguns were found at the centre. The guns were in fact used to ward off wild animals.

Jon Melzack was seriously injured in the raid. Half of his stomach had to be removed and his legs were badly damaged. Jon's twelve-year-old daughter Phoenix was also seriously hurt. Phoenix was placed in a local hospital where she caught the Ebola virus from a dirty needle. Three days later, her mind overwhelmed by the hallucinations the virus causes, she jumped into a river and was swept away.

Despite his wounds, Jon was transported by the Americans to a 'Black Site' prison in Afghanistan. He was frequently tortured by CIA officers and their Afghan colleagues who continued to believe he was a terrorist.

Following his release Jon launched a lawsuit in the International Criminal Court of the Hague. The Americans agreed to pay ten million dollars in damages on the condition that Jon did not talk to the press about his treatment. Jon used the compensation to establish the Mission for Peace and Reconciliation in Surrey, UK.

I take a long slow breath.

I think about Melzack's biography, and particularly about his daughter catching Ebola. Was that the blow that unhinged him? Or was it the years of false imprisonment that twisted him into a cold-hearted killer who could plan the deaths of thousands of children?

Then I open the video file, which has the title AFRICA 2010.

It takes me a few seconds to tune into the visuals. The scene is one of chaos and smoke. I see the shattered remains of huts and buildings. It is a camp, I realise. A wobbly tracking shot. Soldiers are patrolling, laughing as shots are fired. The accents are American, the words often indistinct. There are bodies lying on the smoking ground.

Melzack's camp – just after the drone attack? It has to be. A soldier walks into the shot. He has a small American flag on his uniform. He stands over a woman. Her body is shattered but she is still trying to move.

'Hey Sam! I got a crawler here.'

'That's his wife,' says a voice off camera. 'Waste her.'

He places a gun to the woman's head. And kills her with a single shot.

Then the camera angle changes, spinning to the left. In the dense jungle next to the camp it seems the photographer has noticed something. The shot zooms in and the trees shake as someone, or something, moves away fast.

The video ends. I spool back a couple of seconds, freezing the image just as the photographer zoomed into the vegetation.

A face is there. Deep in the shadows. The outline of a girl's face. A twelve or thirteen-year-old girl. Only just visible. Buried deep in the undergrowth. Staring eyes. A blank look of horror.

Was it Melzack's daughter, Phoenix? Had she just witnessed the soldier killing her own mother?

I write a quick email to Tanya thanking her for the files.

Then I forward them both to Cora.

Finally I turn off the light and seek oblivion. Sleep is the only place I can find peace.

It doesn't last long. At 3 a.m I am awake, the images of Melzack's video churning in my mind.

'A crawler.'

'Waste her.'

The casual slang of an atrocity in action. Little wonder that Melzack has so much success in recruiting members. He's been handed the ultimate radicalisation tool.

Then those eyes. Deep in the darkest part of the undergrowth. Watching the whole scenario play out. Melzack's daughter. Soon to be hospitalised, later to die of Ebola.

Phoenix.

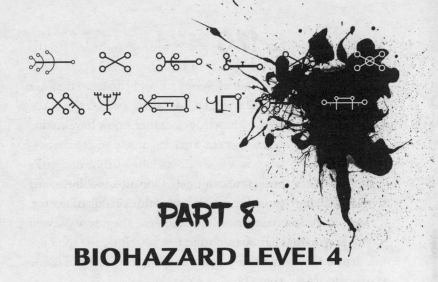

PART 8
BIOHAZARD LEVEL 4

Patrick Eden: He's ripping files off the shelves. He's gathering papers on the floor. (Sounds of banging, fist on glass.)

Police Command: Leave the facility, Dr Eden. There's nothing you can do on your own.

Patrick Eden: He's bringing out a lighter. He's lighting a fire! He's setting fire to the papers!

Audio transcript from helmet mic worn by Patrick Eden, UK Government bioweapons inspector following emergency call at SYMBARON lab, Hampshire.

The night passes in a kaleidoscope of nightmares. Then Liz and I hit the road to the hospital. My whole body feels on super alert, tense with the knowledge of what I now have to do.

I have a small digital camera with me, ready to get the evidence.

Can I pull this off? How can I get to be alone in the room with Dad? There's still a thousand ways this can all go wrong.

'Back on the merry-go-round,' Liz says.

The pressmen are clustered together, watching the road for our arrival. They're certainly going to get a story later on today if my plan works out.

I look for Joe. It's a relief to see him standing next to the pack of photographers. He got away from the Dog Poisoner! Somehow I never really doubted he would.

We park up outside the hospital where the pressmen immediately start their daily ritual.

Joe and I make eye contact. He's looking white-faced and destroyed – like he's also had a terrible night.

As soon as he sees me he comes close and says, 'Can I talk with you please?'

And I want to talk with him. I really do. And he does look desperate. But right now I've only got the evidence on my mind and besides, Liz counters with, 'Leave her alone, will you?' And she pulls me away.

127 JOE

I follow them up the road. Towards the entrance.

'Just give me two minutes,' I beg. 'That's all I need.'

Becca turns, and I can tell from her eyes she wants to speak.

'Get back to your cleaning!' the driver snaps.

Then she takes Becca firmly by the arm and leads her into the hospital. It's so frustrating but what can I do? I'll just have to try again when she comes out.

I shuffle back to the wall and scrub away at the last letter of the graffiti for a bit. After a while I decide to sneak a peek over the top. I know Becca is in there with her dad so it'll be my last chance to see what's happening.

I climb carefully up the ladder and take a look over.

There she is. Keeping guard. She's been a good daughter. Here every day. For a moment I try to imagine how I would have been if it had been my dad. And I know I would have done the same.

In a way we've both lost our dads; hers to a coma, mine to a prison cell.

Makes me feel closer to her.

I am awaiting my chance. Sitting with my dad, reading pages out loud from *I Claudius* – one of his all-time-favourite books.

Then I make my move.

'I'm really sorry,' I tell the duty nurse. 'I've got the most terrible headache. Is there any chance you could get me a couple of paracetamol?'

'No problem. I've got some in my locker. Be back in a moment.'

As soon as the nurse leaves the room I get to work. I know I'm likely to have less than a minute before she's back so I act fast. I take out the camera. I move to the stand that holds the intravenous drip. The false sticker is still there. They must replace it with a new one each time the sachet of pentobarbitone is changed.

I flick at the edge, peeling it back. But my fingers are shaking, and the sticker rips. I pause, fearing that the nurse will even now be walking back down the corridor.

How long have I got? Thirty seconds? Maybe a bit more, I don't know. The corridor must be about fifteen metres long so ...

Don't think about it. Get on the case girl. Do it *right*!

129 JOE

The nurse goes out of the room. Becca quickly stands up and she's got this camera in her hand. She starts to mess around with the drip her dad's connected to and I wonder what she's up to.

Suddenly a vehicle zooms down the road behind me. I turn for a moment, just to check it's not Derek, and that's when I catch movement in the corner of my eye.

Six stories up. A shifting shadow again in the unfinished office block. There's a figure there, just like before. The same one dressed in black. And this time I can see who it is as clear as day because he's staring into binoculars and not taking any notice of me.

My friend, the Dog Poisoner.

The man I hate above anyone else on this planet. He's back again, watching the scientist's room. Spying. Just like I am.

And I think back to the notebook he stole, and the connections to the mission and that man Melzack, and I would just love to know how it all threads together. Because I'm sure it does. Somehow. And I know my dad wasn't interested in listening to me but I really must talk to someone soon or I'll go nuts.

I turn back to Becca. She's still doing something with that drip.

I start on a different corner of the sticker. And this time I do it better, peeling the label back in a smooth movement that reveals the true content information underneath.

I frame up the camera. Flick it to macro to get the close up. In the little LCD screen I can see the word PENTOBARBITONE.

The evidence. Irrefutable. Click.

And then I hear the door swing open. And my heart just about slams through my ribs. I whip round, expecting to see the nurse, but it's Liz.

I feel the room spin as all the blood drains out of my head.

She takes in the scene with animal intelligence, looking at the camera, the sachet with the sticker hanging off and figuring it all out in an instant. There is this most terrible pregnant pause.

'What do you think you're doing?' she says.

A moment later she is striding across the room.

'I think you'd better give me that camera.'

131 JOE

Straight away I see that something's kicking off in the room. Becca is trapped in the corner next to the bed. That woman driver is holding her hand out for the camera.

Becca looks freaked out; she's backing her way towards the door. The driver's insisting. Becca's refusing, but looking terrified at the same time. Her hands are behind her back.

My heart is thumping. I wish I could go to help her. But what can I do?

Then the driver grabs her. And Becca's trying to struggle free. And they're both still mouthing off but I can't hear the words through the glass. She's putting up a good fight but the driver wrestles the camera off her.

The woman driver blurts some words into a walkie-talkie. Becca takes her chance. Runs to the door. The driver clutches at her hair, but Becca is surprisingly fast.

Now I can't see them. I scan the other windows, desperate for a glimpse of Becca. What's happening? My whole body is tensed up.

An alarm bell goes off. The soldiers look around like they don't know what's happening. Then the door to the main building bursts open.

Becca runs out.

I run blindly across the courtyard, Liz pounding after me.

'Stop her!' Liz calls to the soldiers.

A squaddie tries to grab me. I swerve to the right and miss him. I get to the security zone and jump the barrier in one go.

'Close the gates!' Liz screams.

I zigzag through the security area as the electric gates are sliding shut, just slipping through the gap with a few centimetres to spare.

I run up the road. Heading towards the park. And I have no idea at all what I will do when I get there. And I am trying not to cry but it's really tough to keep the damn tears away.

What will they do with Dad now?

133 JOE

I spin on the ladder. Look towards the entrance. Now Becca's running up the street towards me. The electric gates have slammed shut behind her, stopping anyone following for a few seconds. One of the outside guards is in pursuit but he's too busy yabbering into his walkie-talkie to have much breath for a chase.

I want to help her, somehow. But my mind is zapped by the speed everything's happening.

Becca shoots across the road and vanishes into the woodland on the edge of the park.

I hear shouting from the yard. I pop my head back over. The woman driver has been stopped. A man in a white coat is bawling her out.

'You idiot! You know she wasn't to be alone in that room!'

I keep sprinting, heading for the trees on the north side of the park. I duck for cover and flash a look back.

Straight away I see Liz running out of the hospital, ten squaddies alongside her.

I need a better hiding place. Completely wild. I push my way into the thickest brambles.

Liz goes up to Joe. Probably asking him if he saw me go. I know he won't split on me.

I see Joe shake his head and Liz stomps away, her body language leaving me in no doubt she is seriously mad.

I pull back even further into the bushes. Curl myself up into a ball and tuck my head right down between my knees.

135 JOE

So it's all happening now. Chain reaction. Whatever Becca and her driver were fighting about it's kicked off a nice little hornets' nest.

I'm still thinking how I can help. I reckon she's hiding somewhere in the woods across the road.

There's a siren wailing somewhere inside the hospital. There's walkie-talkies zapping off over the other side of the wall and the sound of engines revving as they warm up.

Then something catches my eye: two souped-up Range Rovers cruise slowly down the road.

They're black with tinted glass. I'm sure as sure can be they're the same two vehicles we saw going into the gates of the mission place. And I'm thinking 'that's a bit of a mind blowing coincidence'.

The Range Rovers crawl past. It's like they're checking out the road. Then one of them turns into the top of the park and stops near the gate.

136 BECCA

The seconds tick by.

'Rebecca?'

Liz's voice. Horribly near. I can hear the crunch of her foot-steps on the brittle leaves. She is getting close.

'If you're in there, come out now.'

She pushes her way through the undergrowth. I hear the scratchy rustle of the brambles as she parts them carefully with her hands.

I don't dare breathe.

'Rebecca?'

There is a pause. Then the crack of twigs as she pushes back. Relief floods my body.

I wait for a minute or so then move out of the thicket. I see Liz running fast across the open park, heading towards the housing estate on the other side.

And that's when I see activity over at the gate of the hospital. An ambulance has pulled up there. A stretcher is brought out of the entrance.

It's Dad! They're moving Dad out!

I start to run back towards the road.

137 JOE

I am looking towards the entrance at exactly the moment they bring Becca's dad out on a trolley. The boss bloke is yelling fit to bust. They get her dad in the back of a green army ambulance. Doors clack shut.

I twist round. There's more stuff happening here on the street. A lorry. An enormous truck is coming down the road. Then I see a figure clambering over the security fence which surrounds the unfinished office.

The Dog Poisoner.

The ambulance is pulling away from the hospital gates. A cop car comes round the corner and joins it.

138 BECCA

Two dark Range Rovers pull in next to the trees. The men inside are putting on black balaclavas.

I sprint faster. One of them lifts a shotgun. My heart is ready to explode.

He is loading it with cartridges.

Get there! Jump in the middle of the road if you need to.

Just stop that ambulance from leaving!

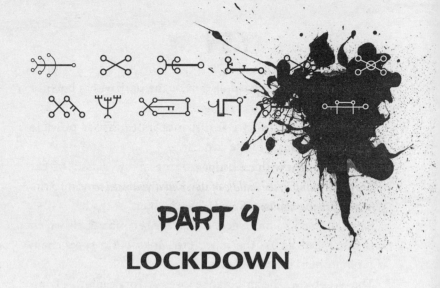

PART 9
LOCKDOWN

Patrick Eden: The lab is filling with smoke. He's staggering towards the glass. Blood is flowing from his mouth, his ears, his eyes ...

Police Command: Do not touch the victim. Repeat, do **not** touch the victim.

Patrick Eden: He's pressing his hands against the glass. His flesh is covered with sores ...

Audio transcript from helmet mic worn by Patrick Eden, UK Government bioweapons inspector following emergency call at SYMBARON lab, Hampshire.

139 JOE

One of the Range Rovers pulls out of the park with a burst of speed you have to see to believe.

It doesn't screw around. It just motors as fast as possible straight into the side of the cop car.

There's a massive great crunch of metal and glass. The car crumples like a Coke can. It skids sideways and slams into the wall. Close enough to me I can feel the blast of the hit.

Same moment, a bloke gets out of the second vehicle which has just raced across the road. He yanks out a spiky chain right in front of the ambulance.

The tyres blow. The ambulance loses it. Totals it into a lamp post. Steam spewing out of the front.

140 BECCA

They've stopped the ambulance!

I just keep running towards it. A gunshot rips through the air.

Two men sprint up. There's a soldier in front. They smash the windscreen with a sledgehammer. Fragments of pulverised glass skitter across the tarmac as shouts ring out.

I see Joe, over by the wall. He's ducking down, wide-eyed with fear. My lungs are bursting.

The back windows of the ambulance crackle as they shatter.

'Rebecca! Get down!' Liz screams, somewhere distant, in the park.

141 JOE

Down by the security gate there's a sudden massive great **blast**!

The huge great lorry has driven into the entrance and exploded. The bang blasts my eardrums. A fireball of heat rolls down the road. I crouch even lower. My body is screaming to run but I'm paralysed, can't move.

They've blocked the entrance to the military place – the whole road in fact – with the burning lorry.

One bunch of guys is attacking the ambulance. Two others climb out of the Range Rover – the one that rammed the cop car – face masks on.

'Armed police!' someone in the crushed car shouts.

He's trying to open the glovebox but the raiders poke a canister in. Spray the cops with this white gas.

Becca! She's crazy! She's running right towards the ambulance!

142 BECCA

Out comes the hospital bed. Dad strapped on. It crashes on to the road, flimsy wheels buckling under the blow.

I'm still running. Almost there. Ten metres to go.

They're ripping at the leather straps. Yanking him off the trolley. Carrying him between them.

I trip. Crash hard on to the tarmac.

A pistol shot rings out. A raider goes down. He *drops* my dad. Hip first on to the steel-hard ground. The second raider dives for cover behind the ambulance.

I stumble forward, grab hold of Dad's legs.

Two more shots split the air. They ricochet off the road near my feet. I see a blur of speed coming towards me.

Joe!

143 JOE

I sprint through the smoke. Through the bullets.

Becca looks at me for a fraction of a heartbeat. Her eyes are flashing with this incredible inner fire.

'Take the other leg!' she orders.

We drag her dad to the Range Rover. Another shot cracks off from somewhere.

'Get him in!' Suddenly, Becca's driver is by our side. She helps us haul him into the back seat. Then she turns back to me.

'Get out of here,' she says, pushing me hard in the chest.

I stumble away from the Range Rover and fall to the ground just as another shot rings out.

144 BECCA

My head snaps to one side in a reflex whipping movement as a bullet zings through the air. The sonic crack sends a percussive blast into my ears. For a split second the air is ruptured. I feel the turbulence against my skin.

The air goes red. Liz gives out a wet groan, a sharp exhalation of air as the bullet rips into her skull.

She slumps right on top of me. As I try to heave her off I hear the dreadful sound of her lungs trying to suck in air.

Then, sirens.

145 JOE

Sirens! Far away but getting nearer.

Across the road there's the sound of an engine kicking up. Voices are yelling.

The truck is still burning by the entrance. No soldiers can get out.

I'm on the ground. I raise my head to see. A wounded raider climbs into his van and drives at crazy speed across the park. Smoke billows everywhere from the crashed vehicles.

Becca?

Then I hear this moaning noise from behind the ambulance. A raider crawls out from cover. He's a massive guy, built like a wrestler. His face mask has come off.

It's the Dog Poisoner.

146 BECCA

Gas enters my lungs. I start to cough, retching as I bring out a handkerchief to cover my mouth. Dad gets it too, his frame shuddering.

Liz has a hole the size of a fist in the side of her head.

My throat goes into spasm. I hear a helicopter coming closer.

Joe. Where's he gone? He was here just a moment ago. Is he OK? I climb out of the Range Rover. The street is so thick with smoke I can't see anything.

Was he shot? Did he run away?

Then I hear a voice through the haze.

147 JOE

The Dog Poisoner starts crawling. I'm following him. He's reaching for a gun which is lying on the ground.

I stand on his wrist. He groans. My heart is beating at a million beats a minute. And now I'm pulling him back with all my force. He rolls over on the pavement. Starts swearing.

I check out the gun. Curved magazine. Gleaming black barrel. And some voice inside me says '*pick it up*'.

So I do. I cradle it in my left hand. It's pointing at his head. 'You killed my dog.' A few more seconds glide past.

And my finger feels like it was *made* to curl round that trigger.

148 BECCA

'Don't you think there's been enough shooting?'

I grab Joe by the shoulder. Snatch the gun out of his hands. He stares at me in a daze for a moment then seems to come to his senses.

I throw the gun so it spins across the road.

'Come on!'

I pull Joe by the hand and we both turn back towards the Range Rover.

Two bodies are lying on the road. Blood and bullet cases litter the tarmac. The air clears a bit. I hear police cars arriving near the hospital entrance. The helicopter is closer still.

Then I realise. The road is still completely blocked by the burning lorry. They can't reach us until they put out the flames. We've got a few more seconds.

And what now? If I knew how to drive, I could just step into the Range Rover and get away with Dad. I turn to Joe.

'Can you drive?'

I check the dash. The keys are in there.

The sirens are closing in. There's a police helicopter coming over the hospital. I have to decide. Decide right now. I can keep out of trouble. Not get involved. Just run away through the park and go home and pretend none of this has happened.

Or I can help Becca.

I stare into her eyes. Those deep blue eyes. Just for a split second.

I tell her, 'get in the car'.

150 BECCA

Joe turns the key and the engine roars into action. The noise of the helicopter becomes intense.

'Come on! Let's go!'

And my mind is just spilling over with the most manic *stuff*. People have been killed. *How* can we just drive away? Are we doing the right thing?

We pull away at high speed. Straight into the woods.

I think about what's been happening. The way they drugged Dad. The scan that lied about his condition. The way I've been controlled. The press manipulation.

I want to bring Dad back to life and hear him talk and laugh. And look me in the eyes and tell me that no way would he commit suicide and leave me alone. And this is the only way.

Joe drives right into the woods.

I snatch a look back. The police cars have broken through the burning barrier.

I zigzag between the trees, steering over bushes and smaller stuff, heading into the thickest part of the woody area.

'What are you *doing*?' Becca hisses. 'Shouldn't we just go straight across the park?'

'Too visible,' I tell her. 'The helicopter might follow us.'

The police chopper rips up the air. The trees are swaying and beating against each other and for a second I think they are following us using a heat sensor or something.

But then it moves away, back to the road where the chaos has kicked off.

I keep under the trees, all the way round the side of the park. Then we come out on to the grass, close to a place where I know we can drive into the estate. There's a few dog walkers around so I keep the speed safe.

'The police are there!' Becca says, looking back.

'Any following us?'

'Don't think so.'

I steer on to the road and we pass through the estate. At the T-junction I take a left, heading for the quiet residential areas to the west.

'Keep going,' Becca says. Her whole body is shaking. I drive through some roads full of terraced houses. Nice gentle pace. We've put a good bit of distance between us and the mayhem before Becca turns to me and says in this small voice:

'We've done it.' Then she starts to sob and I want to put my arms around her.

Then it hits me smack between the eyes. What the *frick* are we going to do next?

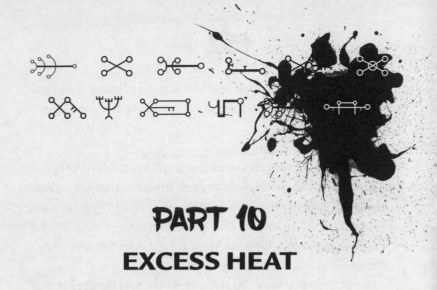

PART 10
EXCESS HEAT

Patrick Eden: Entering the wet zone now. Thick smoke. (Coughs.) Simon, I'm going to get you to the isolation bay.

Police Command: Backup team, ten minutes.

Patrick Eden: OK, I've got a grip on him, his arm around my shoulders. (Coughs.) I can feel the heat of his body even through the suit.

Audio transcript from helmet mic worn by Patrick Eden, UK Government bioweapons inspector following emergency call at SYMBARON lab, Hampshire.

'We have to sort my Dad out,' Becca goes, biting away the tears. 'See if you can find a quiet place where we can stop for a few minutes.'

'OK.'

I crunch the gearbox down into second. Try to keep the speed steady. Don't want to get any more attention, so just cruise, nice and gentle.

Got to admit it. I'm still buzzing from what we've done. Stolen her dad away from beneath their noses! And I'm *with* Becca alone in this car. Well, nearly alone.

But at the same time I'm starting to brick it. Because if they catch us now we are in *so much trouble*. And what about *my* Dad? Is he still in jail? Has he got his heart pills? I really want to see him.

Zebra crossing. I brake to a stop. A woman goes over with a pram. She gives me a puzzled look which quickly turns nasty.

'You need a baseball cap or something,' Becca tells me.

We arrive at a little residential square full of trees. For the moment there's no one around.

'This'll do,' she says.

153 BECCA

I climb into the back seat where Dad is lying prone, still dressed in his hospital gown. His neck is bent over the edge of the seat and the first thing I do is ease his head a bit further back so he won't fall.

'Dad! Can you hear me?' I say. But his lips remain firmly closed. There is not so much as a flutter of his eyes.

He looks horribly pale, like all the life has been drained out of him. The bump on his head is still prominent and swollen. There is a thick smear of blood on his arm where the drip has been ripped out.

'What's actually wrong?' Joe asks.

'He's been drugged. By the government. They wanted to make it seem he's in a coma.'

Joe's mouth flops open. 'That's a bit outrageous isn't it? When's he going to get better?'

'When the drug wears off I guess.'

The truth is I have no idea how long it will take for the effects of the pentobarbitone to disappear. If they ever do really disappear.

Two workmen walk past the car. They catch a glimpse of my father in the back seat and turn to get another look.

'We'd better keep driving,' I tell Joe. 'Let's move.'

I pull away from the square.

We get to traffic lights. It's the first time I've ever done them. But I do OK. Wait for the green. Not stalling the motor when we have to go.

'What was the fight about in your dad's room?' I ask Becca.

'I was getting proof,' she says. 'Taking photos of the drugs they've been feeding him.'

'The driver got the camera, right?'

'Yes. And I'm sure those shots have already been erased. So they can deny everything.'

I hang a left, driving along the side of a sports field and stopping for some old ladies who are waiting to cross the road. Her dad is kind of gasping in the back.

'Those two Range Rovers in the raid were from that mission place we went to.' I tell her.

Becca nods, her face tight with tension.

'That's what I feared. It had to be them.'

'Everyone wants to get their hands on your dad, right?'

'Yes. That's the problem.'

'So what next?' I ask her.

She pulls out her mobile. 'It's time to get help.'

155 BECCA

I select Cora's number from my speed dial. She answers on the second ring.

'How did it go?' she asks eagerly. 'Did you get the pics?'

I run through the details. The fight with Liz. The bungled kidnap operation by Melzack's gang. Joe's surprise decision to help. And the fact that we have Dad with us in this stolen car.

'*Oh my God!* Is he conscious?'

'Not yet.'

'Where are you now? What's the nearest tube?'

'We passed one a little while ago. It was ... Kilburn.'

'I'll be there in forty-five minutes. Don't do anything else until I arrive.'

I cut the call and turn to Joe.

'We need to wait for a while,' I tell him. 'Let's see if we can find a place to park.'

Joe starts to cruise the streets. 'Who did you call?' he asks.

'Cora. She's eighteen. Her father was the person who died right at the start of this whole mess.'

It's a relief to know Cora is coming. Her extra age and maturity is going to be good news if this madness keeps rolling.

I drive. Looking for some sort of corner where we won't be noticed. Kids are being kicked out of school and we get some dodgy looks from a few of them.

'I need to get my dad some clothes,' Becca says. 'Can you pull in over there?'

She points to a charity shop in a small parade. Second-hand stuff.

'I'll be back in a moment,' she says. 'He can't be dressed in these hospital things once he's conscious.'

Becca goes to a cash machine and takes out some money. Then she disappears inside the shop. I'm getting twitchy now. A cop could turn up. See how old I am. See her dad in the back. Then I'm totally nicked. And I'd have let my dad down, big time. And Becca as well.

'All right. I got them.'

Becca crashes into the car and tosses me a baseball cap. She's got a shirt, trousers and shoes for her dad.

I pull the cap on and start driving again.

'How did you get away from the Dog Poisoner?' she asks. 'I saw him coming after you as I got on the train.'

I tell her about the cops. Getting busted for the faults on the motorbike. It's so good to talk that I just can't stop and before I know it I've blurted out everything about Dad getting arrested as well.

'Oh, Joe,' she says. 'I'm so sorry.'

'They're going to send me to Feltham,' I tell her. 'The young offenders place. I might be in there for months.'

157 BECCA

'What about that?' Joe spots a church with a small car park.

We drive into the little parking area. It feels ideal to wait here; only two out of six places are occupied and there's no sign of anyone about. One of the empty bays occupies a dark corner, partly overhung by a willow tree.

'That'll do.' Joe manoeuvres the Range Rover into the corner and turns off the engine.

I check my dad. He's still somewhere between unconsciousness and sleep, but he looks comfortable for the moment and his breathing is regular. Then I climb back into the front and take my seat next to Joe.

Everything goes quiet. The overhanging branches are shielding us with green light. It's like being in our own secret den. I turn to look at Joe at the same moment he turns to look at me. Our eyes meet, a wave of heat ripples through me for a second or two.

A further minute of excruciating silence drags by. I bite the inside of my cheek as the impulse to reach over and hold his hand becomes ... almost ... irresistible.

'Can I ask you a question, Joe?'

'Sure,' he says.

'Why did you do it? Help me, I mean.'

I think for a while. A weird kind of lump seems to have suddenly grown in my throat. I can swallow, but only just.

'There was this time,' I tell her, 'back at the hospital, when my dad was helping me with the cleaning. You were walking towards us and you looked like your world had just ... just been exploded into little pieces.'

'I remember that moment,' she says quietly.

'And it made this connection inside me. And inside my dad as well. We'd both seen the same look on my Mum's face. When they told her there was no way out ... from the cancer.'

Becca turns towards me. Her eyes have that shiny, blurry look that says tears are on the way.

'And I didn't want you to be alone. To feel like it was you versus the rest of the world and that no one cared.'

Becca rests her head against my shoulder and I can smell this clean soapy smell off her hair. It's nice when she's so close. Her hand curls into mine. Her fingers feel incredibly soft and warm.

'That was the time when those flowers got ruined,' she says gently. 'They were for your mum, weren't they, Joe?'

'Yeah.'

We are quiet for a few minutes, just thinking. Then her grip tightens on my hand and the tone of her voice hardens.

'What about that gun, Joe? What would have happened if I hadn't taken it away from you?'

159 BECCA

Joe lets go of my hand. He runs his hands through his hair then stares blankly out of the front windscreen for a few minutes.

'I don't know,' he whispers, finally. 'I don't know what I was thinking.'

'Would you have shot him?'

Joe twists to face me. His eyes seem darker than ever. His brow is furrowed with lines.

'He killed Shammy, Becca, poisoned him ... got Dad arrested.'

Joe's voice cracks up.

'The gun felt right,' he continues. 'Felt right in my hands. My finger was getting tighter on the trigger.'

'You were trying to scare him,' I say, needing the reassurance. 'Wasn't that it?'

'Maybe. But maybe ... more.'

'Oh.'

A tear tracks down his cheek. I pull my jumper over my wrist and smudge it away.

'I'm evil too,' he whispers. 'Just like him.'

I look out of the car window, at the net of branches over us. 'Just human', I say. 'It's inside all of us, Joe, don't you think? A dark side?'

'What about the mission?' I ask her. 'You never brought me up to date on what you heard at the window.'

'They're planning a bioweapon attack.' Becca says. 'Part of Melzack's thirst for revenge.'

'Revenge for what?'

'His daughter got Ebola. In Africa. She was injured in an American bombing raid and caught the disease in hospital,' Becca says. 'Now he's planning an Ebola attack on schools where the sons and daughters of US and British military people go.'

'That's sick.'

'The new pathogen is a hybrid,' Becca says. 'My dad reckoned he crossbred it with anthrax so it would be incredibly fast, spreadable through contact in the air, possible to spray from an aerosol can. Thousands of children will be killed.'

Becca twists her hair. Her father makes a coughing noise and she looks back at him.

'We have to stop Melzack,' she says. She looks at me for a long moment. And I know she understands me. I can tell her anything.

'I nearly killed that guy, Becca,' I tell her.

I reach for her. We hold each other tight. Wind rushes through the trees. The willow branches swish against the windscreen.

And I feel so close to her it's like we've melted together.

I check my watch, pulling myself reluctantly away from Joe. I feel like I'm breaking a spell.

'We have to meet Cora,' I tell him.

Joe gets the car going and we hit the streets again. After a few wrong twists and turns we find Kilburn underground station. By chance there's two policemen standing outside. Joe has to raise his arm and pretend to scratch his head so they don't see him.

'We can't stop here,' Joe says.

So we just keep driving round. And while we're doing it my mind is crumbling. About Mum being missing. I'm getting a severe attack of a disease called ...

P-a-r-a-n-o-i-a.

It's the thing about Dad having Mum's address. Going round in my head. Did he see her in the last twenty-four hours before Melzack tried to kill him? She is an expert on vaccines after all. Is it possible he wanted to seek her advice?

The school connection is on my mind as well. How advanced are Melzack's plans to spread Ebola in those schools? The whole thing is crashing out of control. Faster than I can keep up.

Then I snap back to the present. Here comes Cora now. Out of the tube station and she's spotted us right away.

She climbs into the front seat of the car, gives me one of her twisted smiles, and then takes a not-too-friendly glance at Joe. 'How old are you?' she asks.

'Sixteen.'

'I'll drive,' she says.

We swap seats and this girl Cora pulls into the traffic. 'This is pretty radical,' she says. 'Sounds like carnage back there.'

Becca is in the back. She takes a nervous look out of the rear window.

'People were killed,' she says. 'Makes me feel sick to think about it.'

'How's your dad doing?' Cora asks. 'Is he all right?'

'He's breathing OK,' Becca replies. 'But still not out of the coma.'

'It'll take a bit of time, I guess. Now, what's the plan?'

Becca and I swap a look. 'There isn't one,' Becca admits.

'All right. First things first, turn off your mobiles,' Cora says. 'They might be able to track you. Second, where's this vehicle from?'

'We nicked it from the gang that tried to kidnap her dad,' I tell her.

'Are there cameras there? At the hospital?'

'Lots.'

'Then we have to dump it,' she says. 'The police will have the registration plate.'

'I can steal another one,' I offer. 'I know how to hot-wire motors. My dad's mate taught me.'

'Steal one?' Becca says, her face screwed up.

'You got a better plan?' I ask her.

163 BECCA

We park up in a quiet backstreet. Joe takes a couple of things out of the Range Rover toolkit and slips down the road in search of a car to steal. I hate the idea of it but it's true that every policeman within a thousand miles will have the Range Rover registration by now. We've agreed to give him ten minutes.

Cora turns to me. 'He can get us a car then we have to get rid of him,' she says. 'Who is he anyway?'

I tell her how Joe and I met. 'He helped me. I couldn't have got Dad away without him.'

'Well, he's just a complication now,' she says. 'We'll drop him off at a tube station.'

A terrible sadness overwhelms me. I can't help thinking, well ... this is it. There's no reason I'll see Joe again. He'll slip back through the streets to be locked away at Feltham, and Cora and I will head off in a totally different direction. To a fate that is at this moment in time just about as uncertain as it can be.

And how weird is this? I know it's right that he leaves now. But it just feels totally wrong. Going on without him I mean.

Cora must read the look on my face.

'You can't afford to be sentimental,' she says. 'We don't need him and that's it.'

And a part of me knows she is right. And a part of me feels she is so wrong.

We might not need him. But somehow, *I* do.

I pick a small alleyway with a few cars parked up. There's a Ford Focus which looks like it hasn't been moved for months, the windscreen sticky with sap from the tree it's sitting under. I take a shifty look round then smash the back window with a bit of paving stone.

The hot-wiring gets complicated. I keep sparking the wrong wires off each other. My fingers are bleeding a bit with cuts from the glass. Then I find the right cables and the engine starts up. Five minutes later I'm back with Becca and the other two and we're brushing the glass pieces off the back seat of the Focus and getting her dad in.

'We're going to drop you off at an underground station, Joe,' Cora says.

'Oh.'

'We don't want you to get in any more trouble,' Becca says. She's keeping her voice soft, trying to give it to me nicely but she doesn't sound convincing. 'If you leave now you can get out of this and after a few questions and a bit of fuss you can get back to your normal life.'

'But where are you going to go?' I ask her. 'And what if you need my help when you get there?'

Becca can't look me in the face.

'What do I tell the police?' I ask.

'You'll have to bluff it out,' Cora says. 'Think about it, Joe – you had a perfectly legal reason to be there. Then all the shooting and mayhem started up. And you were terrified and wanted to escape.'

'And what? I didn't even *notice* the girl and the unconscious bloke in the back of the car?'

165 BECCA

He looks at me with those burning eyes. I haven't learned to read him. Yet. And now he's gone all quiet, just staring, dead moody, out of the window.

We're getting rid of Joe. It's like a stone in the middle of my chest.

'You understand, don't you?' Cora asks.

'Yeah. I get it,' he replies.

At that moment an *Evening Standard* delivery van pulls up at a newsagent's across the road.

'That's the early paper,' Cora says. 'We should take a look.'

I get out of the car and hurry over to take a free paper. And I suppose I'm expecting to see something along the lines of: 'Gun fight outside hospital. Weapons scientist missing after dramatic kidnap attempt.'

Instead, on the front cover is this:

RIVAL DRUG GANGS FIGHT OUT DEADLY TURF WAR ON LONDON'S STREETS

Underneath the headline is this colour photograph of the battle zone. It shows a number of vehicles and bodies scattered around the tarmac. Prickles run right down my spine.

I show the paper to Cora and Joe.

Becca reads the paper out loud.

'An armed police response unit was scrambled to north London earlier this afternoon after four gang members were killed in what police are calling the capital's worst ever drugs-related incident.'

'It was nothing to do with drugs!' I say.

'We know that,' Becca says. 'But the rest of Britain doesn't.' Then she turns the page and gasps.

'Joe! It's you. There's a photo of you!'

'What?' I snatch the paper off her and take a look. There's a grainy shot, obviously taken by a security camera at the scene of the attack. It's the moment when I picked up the gun, so I look like a right gangster.

Me, holding a gun.

I get an immediate terror inside me. 'What will my Dad think when he sees it?'

She reads on: *'"There are two members of the gang on the run."* a police spokesman commented at a hastily convened press conference. *"The first is Joe Fontana. He may be just sixteen years old but he is a dangerous individual, from a family with well-known links to organised crime."'*

'That is so unfair!' I yell. 'What are they trying to do to us?'

167 BECCA

I keep reading.

'"We are urging the public to keep a look out for a dark Range Rover and advising people not to approach Joe Fontana as he may be armed. His accomplice is a teenage girl, approximately five-foot-eight with long reddish hair. We are still trying to confirm her identity.

'"We have one message for these two teenagers," the police spokesman added. "Give yourselves up immediately at the nearest police station. It's only a matter of time before you are caught."'

I put the paper down. There is this awful silence in the car.

'Why don't they tell the truth?' Joe asks. 'Why are they blaming me?'

'They want to hush the whole bioweapons angle up,' Cora says. 'If they admit they've lost Rebecca's dad, the whole thing will go ballistic. So they've shifted the focus on to *you* instead.'

'But reporters will spot the lies,' Joe blurts out. 'Won't they?'

'Not necessarily,' Cora continues. 'And even if they do, the government can pressure newspapers into not publishing. It's called a D-notice.'

'So I'm stuffed,' Joe says.

There's a sudden knocking on the window. All three of us jump out of our skin. But it's just a traffic warden. 'There's no waiting here,' she tells us. Her eyes widen as she sees Dad in the back.

Cora puts the car in gear and pulls away fast.

'We need fuel,' she says. 'The tank's nearly empty.'

We stop at the first petrol station to fill up. Cora goes off to pay. I'm left alone with Becca and it's that awkward type of vibe you get when no one knows what to say.

Finally I have to break it.

'D'you still want me to leave?'

She chews at the nails on her left hand, staring out of the window.

'No,' she says, finally.

'I mean, you know, I don't want to hang around where I'm not welcome,' I tell her. 'This girl Cora isn't exactly my number one fan is she?'

Becca smiles a kind of sniffy smile and pulls a tissue from a box on the dash. Then she turns to me.

'We can't abandon you now,' she says. 'Not after the way they've manipulated that photo. They've made you the number one target out of all this and it's just not fair.'

'None of this is fair. Not for you either.'

'So we need to clear your name. Find a way to tell the world you're not some violent criminal.'

She puts her hand on mine. Cora returns at that moment and Becca tells her, 'Joe's staying.'

Cora's face twists into a frown and she's about to speak her mind but then something happens that *none* of us are expecting.

Becca's dad wakes up a bit. At least for a second or two.

Dad half opens his eyes:

'The Ice House,' he says weakly. 'Quickly, Becks. A matter of life and death … '

And that's all he says. Before slipping into a choking fit.

But he *was* conscious for a few seconds. And I want to shout and jump for joy because he has spoken those first vital words.

'What's the Ice House?' Joe asks.

'It's my father's secret lab,' I tell him. 'Hidden in a quarry in our garden.'

I hug Dad close, willing the fit to ease. 'Water,' I say. 'He needs water.'

I see a small store nearby. 'Pull in here please, Cora.'

I rush into the shop and buy a bottle of water. Dad turns his head away when he feels the plastic against his lips. He swats the bottle away and it falls and spills. It's like trying to get a toddler to take something they don't want.

Dad coughs long and hard.

'I'll get another,' Joe says.

'Be quick,' Cora tells him. 'And don't use your mobile whatever happens.'

'Yeah. I know.' Joe leaves.

Cora gives me a quizzical look. 'We can trust him, can't we?' she says.

'Of course we can,' I tell her. And I mean it.

I pick up a bottle of water and stand in the checkout queue. Then I see the small TV playing behind the counter. It's me. The picture on the screen is me. Holding the gun.

The shop starts to turn. I feel physically sick. I glance at the other customers, pull my baseball cap low across my face. And that's what decides me. I really need to speak to Dad. Tell him that this news stuff isn't true. I mean, I know I promised not to call. But just one tiny, titchy one ...

After all, think of all those millions of people using mobiles. How can they trace one little handset from all that mess of signal? And even if they can, it's got to take them ages. Hasn't it?

Dad doesn't even know I was almost shot today. About seven times. I need to find out if they let him home yet. If they gave him bail.

There's a cafe next door. I go into the toilet at the back, take out my phone. Then I get second thoughts. I don't want to let Becca down ... but I think about my name and my photo being everywhere. Stuff like that hangs around on the internet for ever. Anyone will be able to google my name. See all this bad stuff. And it'll never go away.

Maybe Dad can help me to sort it all out. Someone has to get the police to stop telling lies. Just a tiny call. I'll make it quick.

I press the button to switch on my phone.

'He's taking too long,' Cora snaps. 'We should leave without him.'

'He'll be right back,' I protest. 'Just one more minute.'

I look at Dad. He is falling unconscious again.

Cora brings a sheet of paper out of her bag. It's the one with the symbols from the Ice House, the one she questioned me about in the British Library.

'Have you done any more thinking about this code, Rebecca? We could have another go at it, don't you think?'

She thrusts the sheet into my hands. 'I don't know,' I tell her. 'I haven't thought about it again to be honest.'

'Think about the types of codes your dad used, Rebecca. How did his mind work when it came to this type of thing?'

I hand the paper back with a firm shake of my head. Cora takes a long and theatrical look at her watch.

She says, 'I just don't want this whole thing to be blown wide open because of some sort of stupid puppy love.'

'Give him thirty seconds,' I reply. 'He'll be with us in a moment, honest.'

He answers after two rings.

'*Dad?*'

'Joe! Thank God you called. I've been bouncing off the walls I'm so stressed. I'm not supposed to have a mobile here but for some reason they just gave me mine back and ... '

'Dad. There's not much time. I've just got to tell you ... '

'What's happening, Joe? I don't get it. It's like the world's gone mad. They've given me the paper. It's you with that gun isn't it?'

He's talking so fast I can hardly hear the words. His voice is fuzzy and strange. Like he's been crying.

'I haven't slept, Joe. They won't give me bail. I'm going mental over all this.'

I rest my cheek against the cool glass of the window. He's still being held. I won't see him today. Or any day soon by the sounds of it. Knowing about his condition makes it worse. The fact he could collapse with a heart attack at any moment.

He sniffs a bit, then he goes, 'You've got to come and see me, Joe. When can you come in?'

'Don't know. There's stuff happening. I can't tell you on the phone.'

Then I notice something I really don't want to see. A sleek black car with two men inside is cruising slowly down the road towards us.

Seconds later they are parking up outside the cafe. And the one in the passenger seat has some sort of handheld scanner.

'That's *them*,' I say quietly. And my heart rate trebles in the space of two seconds. 'They've found us!'

I force myself to quell the panic, remind myself that they will be looking for a girl and a boy in a Range Rover and not a woman and a girl in a Focus.

'Not us. Him,' Cora says. And her voice is dripping pure acid. 'He's turned his mobile on.'

Cora trips the engine into life and slams the Ford into gear.

'That's it,' she says. 'We can't wait for him.'

We pull out into the road.

Another car parks outside the cafe. The men are putting on gas masks.

Oh Joe! What have you done?

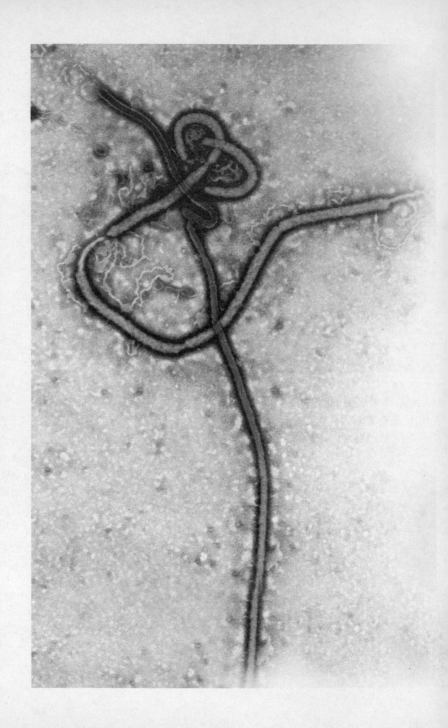

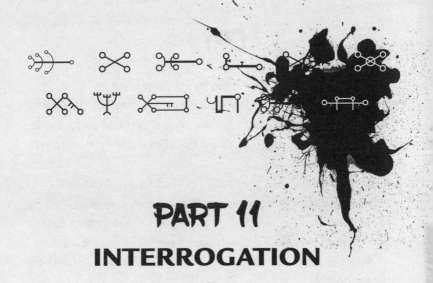

PART 11
INTERROGATION

Patrick Eden: Simon, can you understand me? Lie down on the bed! He's kicking. I'm going to restrain him.

Police Command: You can't save him. Leave immediately.

Patrick Eden: His face ... his face is changing, collapsing, the collagen dissolving.

Audio transcript from helmet mic worn by Patrick Eden, UK Government bioweapons inspector following emergency call at SYMBARON lab, Hampshire.

One second the window is there. The next it's not.

I spin away. Darts of glass punch into my cheek. A dark green canister comes flying through the jagged gap and clatters into the corner of the toilet. I can see this thin trail of yellow smoke coming off the top.

'What's that noise, Joe? Joe ... ?' Dad's still on the line.

Then the stun grenade goes off and I don't know if I'm up, down, spinning around, or hanging from the ceiling by my toes because it's like my brains have been blown out of my nose.

A soldier dressed in black comes in from the cafe so fast he's just a blur.

He body slams me to the floor. I hit the tiles hard. My arm gets twisted behind my back. I think about Becca – send her a message in my mind:

Run! Get out now!

175 BECCA

I've lost it by the time we hit the end of the road. I've held back the emotion for so long but this new blow just hits me too hard and suddenly I'm blubbing like a baby and two tissues are wet through before we reach the North Circular Road.

Joe didn't deserve any of this. All he did was try and help me, out of the goodness of his heart. Now he's been named as a dangerous criminal. And captured by a bunch of government thugs.

'What will they do to him?' I ask Cora.

'May be better not to know.'

I get this sudden stabbing vision of Joe, tied to a bench in a cell, being waterboarded or worse. They are bound to interrogate him. How far will they go? And how long can he hold out for? That, now, is the big question.

Oh Joe. I am so sorry.

There's an iron fist on the back of my neck. Another soldier runs in. My wrists get clamped together with some sort of band. Hands are running through my pockets.

'Give me my mobile!' I yell. I can see it, battery spewed out, lying on the toilet floor. One of them shoves it in a plastic bag.

Now I'm getting dragged through the cafe and there's this bloke in an apron by the coffee machine.

'Who is he? What's he done?' he yells. But it's echoey and far away and I'm not sure I'm really hearing it.

We exit the cafe. And it's like I come out of this tunnel in a big rush.

Have they got Becca? Did she get away?

Then they chuck me in the back of a van.

We are speeding out of London. I've told Cora to head for home so we can get into the Ice House as quickly as possible. And I'm wondering how those government men got to the cafe so fast.

Then I get it: not only did I turn on my mobile earlier, I took out some money as well. I used the cash machine at the shopping arcade where I bought the charity clothes.

They could have traced either, that's how they knew what part of town we were in. Now I feel even worse and I get this phenomenal pang of guilt. Because at least I'm still free and I have someone by my side as backup. But Joe is captured and alone.

'If he cracks,' Cora says, 'they'll be waiting for us when we get to your house.'

'He won't crack,' I say.

Cora gives me a mean look.

'Yeah, right. Like you *knew* he wouldn't turn his mobile on.'

There's a fat bloke in a tie sitting in the back of the van. He looks like a football manager, he's that slimy.

'What about the girl?' Slimeball snaps. He's talking to the men in black.

'Not in the cafe, sir.'

'And the Range Rover?'

'Negative.'

That narks him off. 'Seal the area,' he goes. 'Five-hundred-metre cordon. Black Range Rover. Now!'

The soldiers split up and run off and I'm left with this bloke. He takes out a packet of tissues and hands them to me so I can wipe blood away from my cheek.

'My name is Benson, Joe. Mr Benson to you. Now, where's the Range Rover?'

'Dunno,' I sniff loudly. My head still feels like it's a bell and it's got one of those clapper things in it. 'How should I know?'

Benson. I remember Becca mentioning this guy.

'The girl, Rebecca. She has to be with the Range Rover – with her father.'

He jabs at my forehead with his finger with each word.

'Where – is – she?'

179 BECCA

We make it to the outskirts of London. I just can't stop thinking about what they might be doing to Joe.

More than twenty miles to go and I've already chewed my nails to the quick. Some types of stress are supposed to be good for you but I know for sure that this type isn't.

Dad suddenly starts making these horrifying sounds. Like a series of grunts, as if his chest is being crushed.

I lean over; mop sweat away from his brow.

'What's wrong?' I ask him urgently. 'Dad?'

His breathing is ragged, urgent inhalations through a gaping wide mouth. Then his legs go into this violent kicking movement.

'It's a convulsion!' I tell Cora. 'What can I do?'

A walkie-talkie crackles. A report comes in.

'OK,' Benson goes. 'We're building a picture here, Joe. Pieces of the jigsaw are falling into place. You've dumped the Range Rover in Kilburn.'

'Whatever.'

'So now I'm thinking that maybe you dropped them off somewhere,' Benson says. 'Someone's flat? A private house? A friend of Patrick Eden?'

'Can't remember. That stun thing has made my brain go weird.'

There's a bunch of kids gawping into the back of the van. One of them brings out his mobile. Snaps a pic. Benson loses his rag, slams the back door in the kid's face.

'Back to DHQ!' he shouts at the driver.

Seconds later we're on the go.

181 BECCA

I put my fingers to Dad's wrist. His heart is racing like a piston. Then his upper body goes into a second convulsion, more forceful and frightening than the first.

'It's probably a withdrawal symptom,' Cora says. 'His body's been overloaded with so much barbiturate he's gone into a fit. All we can do is wait for it to pass.'

I dampen a handkerchief in water and dab it against his forehead.

Finally the seizure eases off, but one thing is now clear: there's virtually no chance Dad will be conscious by the time we get to the Ice House. Which means it is up to me to crack that code before we get there; the code that will open that mysterious door.

I take out the paper and get to work.

Time's rolling on. Benson has spent the whole journey barking instructions into his radio. And fixing me with this evil look.

Then the van turns off the road and I see this fighter plane sitting on a concrete block. It's some kind of RAF base.

We get checked through security. I can hear helicopters buzzing about.

'Over there,' Benson tells the driver. He pulls up at this building next to some big hangars. It's a sinister-looking grey block with no windows at all. I'm pulled out of the van and taken inside to a small room which contains a table and two chairs and nothing else.

'Right!' Benson slams the door. 'We're staying in here until you give me the information I need.'

He leans in close to me. The smell of his sweat pricks my nose.

With every passing mile I can feel the pressure build. I have to crack the code before we get to the Ice House.

And time is running out.

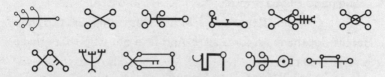

Beneath the symbols I have the list of stars that they refer to.

Polaris, Capella, Spica, Arcturus, Sirius, Vega, Alphecca, Procyon, Deneb Algedi, Regulus, Gienah, Antares.

I start to look for words that spring out of the combination. SAG. SAP. SAD. CRASS. GRASP. GRASS. CRAP.

There's not enough variety in the vowels to make any lengthy words. Too many As and not a single E, I, O or U.

Come on girl!

The door crashes open. A woman rushes in. 'We've been monitoring all the road cameras around the Kilburn area,' she says. 'We got something.'

She hands him a photo.

'That's the girl,' Benson says with satisfaction. 'Get the plate details out there. All force alert. And find out who that vehicle is registered to.'

'Right away, sir.' The woman leaves the room.

'They've switched to a Ford Focus, Joe. So, this is where you come into it: where are they going? And who is the girl who's driving? These are the last tiny pieces of the jigsaw.'

'I dunno.'

'You must know!'

Benson is getting wound up good and proper. He's pacing up and down. He looks massive and scary in this little room.

'Where are they going, Joe?'

'Ten miles to go,' Cora says.

We're really getting close. My panic levels are rising.

I've tried loads of different possibilities and I still haven't cracked the code. Ideas based on distances to the different stars on the keypad. Thoughts exploring words I think Dad might have used. Combinations based on family birth dates and names of pets. But nothing feels right.

Then I remember that curious word scribbled in chalk on the wall next to the metal door:

FIZZES

What if that is somehow a clue? A play on words or a mathematical code that will solve the mystery? It certainly *feels* like a code.

FIZZES

I write down the letters one by one and figure out the number of the alphabet that each one is linked to. 6, 9, 26, 26, 5, 19

I stare at it.

Come on, girl. Get your mind in gear!

186 JOE

The door opens and this younger bloke comes in. 'All set,' he says. He gives Benson a laptop.

'Have a look at this, Joe,' Slime says. He clicks on the space-bar and a video clip kicks off.

It's the CCTV at the hospital. They've zoomed right in. The shot is *just* the Dog Poisoner and me – nothing more.

First thing I get is how clear you can see me. There's nothing fuzzy about this – not like the shot in the paper. And it feels *so* real. Because so far it *is* real.

I'm stamping on his wrist. Then I pick up the gun. And I look like I really know what I'm doing. The Dog Poisoner is holding up his hands like he's begging, 'Don't shoot me!'

Then the gun jerks in my hand. There's even a puff of smoke. Blood spurts.

And my heart just about stops with the shock.

What the ... ?

FIZZES.

I have to put myself in Dad's head to get this. OK. *Fizz.* That's a word in its own right. Maybe this is the way to break down this conundrum, turn one word into two.

Fizz. Can mean bubbles. Or gas. Or pressure. Or something burning like the fuse on a stick of dynamite. Or slang for Champagne.

Es. Spanish for 'is'? Dictionary pronunciation for S? Not that that helps at all. Then I remember that ES is used as shorthand for Spain. As in ESpaña.

Fizz for champagne. Es as in España? Is there a connection there or is my brain just teasing me?

Then my mind trips forward and I have it: *Spanish champagne.* Otherwise known as CAVA.

Yes!

Capella. *Arcturus.* *Vega.* *Alphecca*

I'm not 100 per cent sure that it's right, but it's the best I've got.

As far as this video's showing, I've pulled the trigger! The Dog Poisoner's head slams back with the impact. You can even see the hole in his face. And then comes the blood. Digital blood – I know that. But no one else would.

Benson slowly closes the laptop. But I've got to say something because there's this anger in me like nitroglycerine.

'I never killed anyone.'

'Didn't you Joe? I'm not so sure. I can only believe what I see with my own two eyes, Joe. Just like a jury would.'

He leans forward. His face is close enough I can feel the heat of his manky breath.

'What about your dad, Joe? You know how dangerous it is for his heart to get stressed, don't you? Just imagine how he'd feel if he knew about this murder? Found out his own son was a killer?'

My hands clench into two tight fists. I want to launch myself across the table and smash his smug face in.

189 BECCA

Two miles to go. I direct Cora through the network of lanes, threading a route to the woodland at the back of the field.

'Here's the lay-by. Pull in here.'

Cora turns into the muddy little parking spot and kills the engine.

'I'll stay here and guard your dad,' she says. 'Good luck.'

I run across the field, using the hedge for cover.

It occurs to me I might be walking into a trap. Last time I was at the house there were still a couple of policemen on watch. Also, the very thought of going back into the Ice House is causing the hairs on my neck to spike. What *was* that spooky noise from behind the door?

Well, I'll find out soon enough.

If the code works.

'What about a lawyer?' I blurt out. 'You can't just call me a killer when I'm not.'

He smiles. 'You've been watching too many American soap operas, Joe. It's true that when you're dealing with the police these things can be done. But we operate to a different system here. It's a bit more ... flexible.'

'You can make the rules up as you go along you mean? Fake videos that tell lies. Well. I'm not going to tell you anything. Even if you torture me.'

Benson laughs. A high, squeaky laugh. Then his mobile pings and he checks the screen. He taps in an answer and fixes me with this intense look.

'We've had news from the place your dad's being held.'

'What? What is it?'

I lean forward in my seat, try to see the little screen.

'It seems that your father's been taken sick, Joe. Something to do with his heart.'

191 BECCA

I reach the woods. Make it into cover. I hide behind a tree and wait for a few seconds to regain my breath.

Stay focused, I tell myself. *Don't let the fear corrode your mind.*

At any moment I'm expecting the silence to be shattered by a shout or a cry as the alarm is raised. But the creaking and swaying of branches is all I can detect.

Going slowly isn't an option. So I move swiftly through the copse, weave a trail through low-lying bushes, keeping away from any paths.

The code runs through my mind, over and over. CAVA. It *has* to be the answer; it's the only thing that fits.

Then I remember that handwritten note on the titanium door, the one about the explosive.

Even if the code works, will the Semtex blow?

'Let me see it,' I tell him. My voice is shaking. My whole body too.

'Very well,' Benson says. He holds the screen up towards me and I see this message:

Joe Fontana's father was taken to Mount Vernon hospital twenty minutes ago with a suspected heart attack.
Currently in intensive care.

My chest tightens until I feel I can hardly breathe. Dad! Oh Dad! Please let this be another lie. It has to be a trap. Doesn't it?

I sit on the chair; hold my head in my hands. If it is true, it's all my fault. I put him under too much stress.

'We're not monsters, Joe,' Benson says. 'We care about you, I promise. Maybe I could run you down to the hospital to see him?'

And I still think it's some sort of trap. But what can I do?

'Yeah – let's go! Now!'

193 BECCA

I get to the quarry and slow my pace. If they've cracked Joe, this is where they might be waiting. I approach it with extreme care, crawling the last few metres and pushing through brambles to take a look.

I scan the high walls of the quarry, looking for movement, or a face ... or the barrel of a gun.

No one's there. It looks OK.

I step stealthily across the quarry and enter the old summer house. Seconds later I am pushing up the tiny hidden catch and the door is swinging wide.

Inside, everything is as it was. Torn apart. Wiped out. A heartbreaking scene of chaos.

I tiptoe carefully through the wreckage and turn on the feeble light, wishing that there weren't *quite* so many shadowy corners in the room.

And there is the polished metal doorway, the lustrous surface gleaming and sleek.

194 JOE

Benson leads me out of the building. We climb into this black Jaguar and it pulls away smoothly.

We drive for fifteen minutes.

'Here we are,' he says. We pull into a hospital.

Benson explains who we are. A nurse leads us down a corridor. All the while I'm getting these flashbacks to the time when Mum was in and out of these places.

All those months. The cancer always there, playing with her, now getting a bit better, now a bit worse. She was cheerful though, never showing when it hurt.

'Intensive care unit 4,' the nurse says. 'This is the one, Joe.'

And there he is. Unconscious. On the other side of the glass. Plugged into cables and tubes.

I want to punch through the window and go to him.

195 BECCA

I study the keypad, my eyes gradually adjusting to the dim light. The symbols are only just visible and I don't want to make a mistake, so I pull the sheet of paper out of my pocket and check I am getting it right.

Capella, Arcturus, Vega, Alphecca. I've had to assume that Dad would use the first two As on the list.

My mouth is completely dry. My fingers shake as I reach forward and press the buttons.

Nothing happens for a second or two and in that awful moment of disappointment I think I've failed. But then the whispering sound of compressed air starts up and the door slides open with a gentle hissing noise.

I take a step back.

Now I can see what is inside this mysterious new space chiselled out of the raw rock. It is a moment so totally loaded with menace that I feel the breath instantly crushed out of me.

The nurse leaves us. I watch my dad for a while through the window. Then Benson turns to me.

'I wouldn't want your dad to have to see that film clip of the murder, Joe,' he says. 'I worry that it might be too much for him.'

His eyes narrow. He brings out a tablet.

'I've got the file of the video clip here, Joe. And I've also got your father's email address.'

He flips the screen towards me. I stare at the email address, a silent scream of rage swirling inside me.

'One little click, Joe, and it will be sitting in his inbox when he next logs in. We can keep you in custody for as long as we like, in a place where you won't be able to speak to him. There'll be nothing you can do to stop him seeing it.'

I stare him out. But I know he's right; if my Dad sees that mocked-up film of the so-called killing then his heart could give up for good and *everything* will turn to crap. For *ever*.

'We can work this all out, Joe, so that *no one* needs to see it,' he says softly. 'The clip will be erased and no one will ever know it even existed.'

I stare at Dad. At the monitors and drips. The bandage across his chest.

'I'll count down from five, Joe, then I'm sending this clip. Five, four, three, two ... '

His finger hovers above the tablet.

'Don't send it!' I hiss. *Oh Becca. I am so sorry.*

197 BECCA

I am expecting it to be a secure storage zone. I am expecting to see virus flasks on shelves.

And there is a shelf with a single virus flask sitting on it. But that's not all ... because on the other side of the dark cavity there is a crumpled figure lying on the rock floor.

It is my mother.

My mother! Lying motionless on the floor. Her face deathly pale. Her chestnut hair pooled around her like an outpouring of blood.

Seconds later I hear the crackle of broken glass behind me. Someone has stepped into the Ice House. A jolt of terror assaults me. I spin around.

Cora.

In her hands she holds a gun. And it is pointing right at my heart. Her face twists into that weirdly fixed smile.

'Nice work, Rebecca,' she says. 'I always had a feeling you would crack that code. You really are a clever girl.'

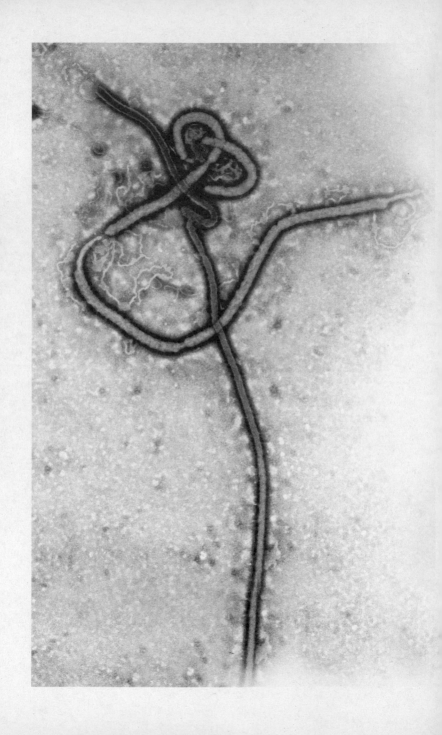

PART 12
SPEED RESPONSE

Patrick Eden: Simon … talk to me! (Coughs.) How did you become infected?

Police Command: Is he speaking? We can hear moans and screams.

Patrick Eden: Oh my God … he just coughed up the mucous lining of his throat.

Audio transcript from helmet mic worn by Patrick Eden, UK Government bioweapons inspector following emergency call at SYMBARON lab, Hampshire.

Soon as I tell Benson what he wants to know, the manic stuff kicks right off. He hustles me out of the hospital and waves to the driver of a Land Rover which is parked up nearby.

It races over and a military guy gets out.

'Bring the choppers in,' Benson says. Within seconds I hear the clatter of helicopters coming in towards the hospital.

'What about him?' the other military man asks, nodding at me. 'Detention cell?'

Four jet-black helicopters fly in fast over the rooftops.

'He's coming with us,' Benson says. 'He might be useful if we get into a siege scenario.'

'Cora ... ?'

The gun doesn't waver. Her hand is rock steady, her eyes glittering like quartz as she stares at me. My breathing becomes shallow as my throat constricts.

'What makes you think I *am* Cora?' she says.

I clutch at the wall to steady myself.

'It surprised me how easy it was,' she says casually. 'All I needed was an email account with her name in it and a pay-as-you-go mobile number.'

I glance at Mum. I'm desperate to go to her.

'You never suspected me at all,' 'Cora' laughs.

A wave of nausea rises inside me. And I'm totally kicking myself. It's true I never thought to track down an image of the real Cora Hazelgrove. And I never called her at a landline, I only ever called her mobile.

I stare at the gun, noticing the natural way she holds it. Like she's done it a thousand times before.

'Who are you? What do you want?'

She shines a flashlight into the dark space. Sitting on a shelf is that small metal object, the only thing the vault contains apart from Mum: the virus flask. Complete with biohazard sticker. She steps inside and takes it.

'I want *this*. Just like everyone else.'

Benson gets approached by two commanders. The helicopters are sitting there, blasting the air as their rotors churn.

'Who have we got at the scientist's house?' he shouts.

'Two armed police,' comes the reply. 'How do you want to deploy them?'

'Get them to recce the quarry at the bottom of the property. If anyone goes in there I want to know about it. But tell them no confrontation; this is a job for a team in full bioprotection suits.'

Benson pushes me into one of the helicopters. I crash on to a seat. Someone clips a seatbelt round my waist. Engines roar as the air is chopped up and mixed by a million rotor slices.

I slam my fists to my ears. Fumes are bunging up my nose. One of the soldiers snaps some headphones on to me.

I hear someone call, 'ETA – seventeen minutes'.

201 BECCA

'Cora' steps towards my mother. I lurch forward, protective instincts kicking in.

'Don't touch her!' I shout.

The girl turns abruptly, swivelling the gun. I stop in my tracks, my heart pounding.

'I know who she is,' she says sharply. 'And don't worry. They want her alive.'

'The mission? You're doing this for Melzack, right?'

Her face locks as she attempts a wry smile. 'Let's say I'm a sympathiser.'

The noise of our conversation has roused Mum. She is alive! She stirs a little, moaning as if coming out of the deepest sleep ever.

'Water ... ' she whispers.

We approach her. Her eyes are opening.

'Water ... please ... ' I rush back into the laboratory, crossing to the smashed-up sink. I pray the tap will still function. It does. I find an intact mug on the floor and fill it with water.

My mother drinks it down in a single draught. Then she gets unsteadily to her feet and we help her towards the door.

So far she has not recognised me.

Inside the helicopter the soldiers are dressing in white biosuits, fitting full facemasks over their heads.

Benson is bringing out a map, unfolding it and talking with the one of the men. The ground is whizzing past at incredible speed.

Deep inside me I have this hot spot of pain; Becca is going to get hurt. And her dad as well. And she's only got me to thank because it's *me* that's blown it. Screwed it right up. Like some snitching little snake, I've ended up giving them *exactly* what they wanted: Becca's head on a plate.

We're flying over green fields and lakes as Benson's walkie-talkie crackles loudly.

'The officers at the house are moving towards the quarry now, sir.'

203 BECCA

We re-enter the larger room of the Ice House. Mum sways uncertainly as she struggles to get air into her lungs. I give her another mug of water and she drinks it fast.

'Take it easy,' I tell her gently. 'Breathe deep. Sip it slowly ... '

For the first time in five years I am holding her in my arms. I force back the tears as she turns to me, her face registering shock, then dazed wonder.

'Rebecca?'

Mum's hand reaches up, strokes my cheek. I feel a catch in my throat as five years of pent-up emotion threatens to flood out.

'Get moving!' 'Cora' says, ramming the gun barrel into my shoulder.

We stumble out of the Ice House into the quarry. My mother is weak and her feet are bare. She puts her arm around my shoulder as we climb up the wooded slope.

'Shhhh!' 'Cora' suddenly drops down, signalling for us to do the same. Through the leaves we see two policemen, twenty metres away, moving stealthily towards the quarry. I think about screaming for help but it's as if she's reading my mind.

'I will kill you both if you make a sound,' she hisses. The menace in her eyes is enough to convince me she really is not kidding. Who *is* this girl? What is her mission? And why is she prepared to kill on Melzack's behalf?

The two men move past without seeing us.

Benson's looking more closely at the map. I can see a house and trees marked. And the senior officer stabs his thumb on this bit marked QUARRY.

'That's it,' he says. 'We go in hard as soon as we touch down.'

Then I'm wondering is there something I can do to help her. Pretend to go crazy. Rush through to the cockpit and try to grab the controls.

But it's never going to work. There's ten of these mean-looking soldiers in this helicopter. They'd stop me before I'd barely got started.

The soldiers are bringing more stuff out of kit bags. Each of them clips into a remote oxygen supply, run from a cylinder on their backs.

'Don't you dare hurt her!' I shout at Benson.

He just smiles and puts his finger to his lips.

205 BECCA

We reach the edge of the field. The car is right in front of us.

I hurry across to the lay-by and fling the rear door open. 'Dad!' A rush of relief courses through me as I see he is tied up ... but alive.

I pull his gag free. Dad gazes at me. He is regaining consciousness with every passing minute. Then he sees Mum.

'Sarah?' he croaks, his eyes lighting up with joy. 'Come to me.' She stays still. I am holding my breath.

Slowly she approaches the car. Her whole body is trembling. She leans into the back of the vehicle.

'I'm so sorry,' she whispers.

It is five years since I've seen my parents embrace.

'This family reunion is all very touching,' 'Cora' says coldly, 'but the clock's ticking and we've got some miles to do.'

She throws the charity clothes to Dad.

'Get dressed.'

As I climb into the passenger seat I hear the distant clatter of helicopter rotors.

'That's them,' 'Cora' says. 'I told you Joe would crack. We have to shift.'

'ETA three minutes,' comes a voice from the cockpit.

The cold is biting now. I'm shivering in my T-shirt and the air is blasting through the open side door.

The soldiers bring out assault rifles. They are loading. Checking. I beat my arms against my sides and blow on my hands to try and warm them. The soldiers don't say a thing. Just do their stuff like robots.

Benson nods to his men. There's a definite rise of tension. The engine noise changes as we start to descend.

'Standby,' Benson calls.

We speed through the lanes towards Melzack's mission centre and, despite the horrific stress of the situation, I can't help but feel a huge surge of love for my parents as I see them together in the back of the car. But at the same time there are questions I desperately need to ask.

'What were you doing in the vault?' I ask Mum.

'I'm so sorry,' Mum says quietly. 'I came to help your Dad with the vaccine. We wanted to tell you ... I wanted to see you, but ... ' Her voice cracks with emotion.

'And the vault?'

'Your father and I were working in the Ice House when these thugs arrived,' Mum says. 'Your father had created a false vial with a dummy virus. A terrible fight started. I did the only thing I could think of to protect the real virus – dive into the vault and let the code protect me.'

We pass a sign. We're not far from Melzack's mission.

'I was trapped,' Mum says. 'After three days, I collapsed with dehydration.'

'We should have been straight with you,' Dad whispers. 'Told you your mum was coming to the house.'

The helicopter banks to the right. Out of the door space I can see a forest, then fields. Cattle run away in panic as the helicopters comes in low.

'That's the place,' Benson says. 'Get the pilots to take us in as close to the quarry as they can manage.'

We zoom over the rooftop of a house. Then the radio goes off.

'The police have found fresh footprints going in and out of the Ice House,' a voice announces.

The helicopter lands and the soldiers vanish into the woods. Benson waits impatiently with two of his deputies. Minutes pass. Then I hear a message on the comms:

'There's no one inside. We're too late!'

'Damn it!' Benson exclaims. 'We have to go to Melzack's mission.'

Five minutes later the troops are back on board. The four helicopters take off, turning sharply over the woods.

209 BECCA

We race through a small village, pushing ever harder down leafy lanes as the mission gets closer.

I turn to the back seat. Dad is now sitting, drinking from a bottle of water. He is gradually getting his wits back and has been staring at 'Cora'. Now he addresses her bitterly.

'You people were trying to kill me five days ago,' he says. 'But Melzack seems to be pretty keen to keep me alive now. What made him change his mind?'

'Your notebook,' she replies. 'He wants you on his team, be a part of his strategy. Dark Heart is just the beginning.'

My father's face goes pale.

'He's got the *notebook*?'

He flashes me a look of utter desolation and I get a terrible stab of guilt.

'He can create the Ebola vaccine by following those notes,' he mutters to Mum. 'Protect himself and his followers while killing whoever he likes.'

A nightmare vision hits me: the thousands of children in those schools. The doors bolted. The virus doing its deadly work.

I close my eyes, wanting to shut away the pain.

210 JOE

The other three aircraft come alongside us as we race away from the house.

'ETA four minutes,' the pilot says through the cans.

We're back on the hunt. Four minutes to the mission centre. Things are moving so fast my brain can hardly keep up. I think non-stop about Becca. Wishing I had some way to contact her.

Benson's got other ideas. He comes and sits next to me, pulling the headphones away from my ear.

'Time for you to make yourself useful,' he says, his voice hard as iron.

He brings out his tablet.

'Here we go,' 'Cora' says. We turn into Melzack's centre, the huge wrought-iron gates parting to let us up to the security hut.

She flashes a pass.

'He's in the Grand Hall,' the gateman tells her as he raises the barrier.

We drive into the complex. There are security guards buzzing around everywhere. Some of them are carrying kitbags. Others are unloading wooden crates from the back of a truck. Sandbag bunkers have been built in front of the buildings.

I see a pile of rifles, partly hidden beneath camouflage netting. It looks like Melzack is preparing for a war.

'Cora' navigates her way through the roadways and we park up next to a huge building.

'Out!' she commands. I help my parents out of the back seat. They are both still shaky on their feet. 'Cora' pushes us towards a doorway.

'In there!' she snaps.

'You've been inside the mission, haven't you Joe?'

He zooms into a map.

'Which one is the lab?'

Now's my chance. To mess them up.

'And if you plan on lying,' he continues, 'just think about Rebecca. People can so easily get killed in friendly fire incidents at this type of raid, Joe. Do you know what I'm saying?'

I do know what he's saying. And I've never hated someone more. Not even the Dog Poisoner.

I point to the place he's asking about. Anything to protect Rebecca. Anything.

Even helping the devil.

213 BECCA

The doors sweep open and we are ushered into a large hall, smoky with incense. Rows of black-clad devotees stare at us as we are escorted down the central aisle. I scan the crowd to see if I can see Tanya but I can't pick her out.

Melzack stands in front of the crowd, dressed in his white robes, his eyes fixed on 'Cora's' hands.

She steps forward and gives him the sample. He takes it with a triumphant smile, then holds it aloft while a woman points a microphone towards his neck.

'You are the ... children of chaos,' he says to the devotees, the robotic squeak of his voice resonating weirdly through the hall. 'The dispossessed ... the refugees ... the true losers ... of the global wars ... our masters perpetuate. Every one of you ... has had a life destroyed ... by American war mongering ... by their British puppets. Well, now we will ... send them a message ... in the only language ... they understand.'

The room erupts in shouts of support. But even as the disciples are punching the air, 'Cora' is stepping forward and whispering urgently to Melzack. The guru's face clouds with concern.

Then I hear turbulence in the air. The helicopters?

Melzack whispers something to his guards. The men pull pistols from shoulder harnesses and run from the hall. A ripple of unease runs through the assembled crowd.

214 JOE

We come in above this big building. I'm wondering about Becca. Is she in there? Is she safe?

Our helicopter banks round. Two of the other aircraft are already dropping guys on to the roof.

'Put us down in front of the building!' Benson shouts at the pilot.

'Incoming!' the pilot yells into the intercom. Sharp impacts thwack into the metal skin. Bullets? The pilot takes evasive action, throwing the helicopter sideways. Every inch of my body trembles. I imagine how a bullet would feel if it ripped into my flesh.

Out of the door I see three guys in black robes running out of the hall. Fire spurts from their guns.

'Take them out!' Benson orders. Two of the soldiers let rip towards the guys on the ground but they dive for cover behind a wall.

I hear the crack of breaking glass.

215 BECCA

The glass panels of the roof explode. Fragments shower on the congregation as screams ring out. Ropes snake down, soldiers rappelling into the hall, throwing stun grenades as they come.

Everyone's panicking. Running for the doors. Melzack's personal bodyguards scatter as half a dozen troops touch down and rush at them.

A series of skull-busting explosions blasts through the hall. An amplified voice calls out:

'Hands on your heads! Weapons on the floor!'

But no one is obeying. The hundreds of disciples are falling over each other in their desperation to reach an exit. Shots go off near the altar. Some of Melzack's men have opened fire.

I push my way through the melee, trying to get to Melzack. I see him snatch up the virus container.

'Those two come with me!' Melzack shouts at 'Cora'. She shoves my parents through the chaos towards him. My blood runs cold. I can't lose them now!

'No!' I lunge out, snatch at her arm. But she turns in an instant and smashes the handle of her pistol into the side of my head.

I stagger backwards, my vision splintering into a thousand glittering stars. Through the haze of pain I see 'Cora' and my parents join Melzack and the Dog Poisoner near a small doorway at the back of the hall.

Then a black cloud engulfs me and I feel myself falling to the ground.

The windscreen is shattered. Then the helicopter shudders.

'Rotor strike!' the pilot announces.

We're hit! Warning lights are flashing in the cockpit. The chopper spins.

The pilot calls, '**Brace! Brace! Brace!**'

We spin faster. Then faster still. I'm hanging on to my seat for dear life, my teeth gritted so hard it feels like they're going to splinter to bits. A two-tone alarm is blasting off.

The engine is spluttering. Smoke comes through the roof. The soldiers hit the floor, spreading their weight across the metal. There's swearing and shouting and Benson's gone green in the face.

The helicopter plummets.

217 BECCA

I'm coming round. On the floor. Strange sounds surround me. I cradle my head in my hands. Pain sears the side of my face.

Feet are running next to me. Someone steps on my leg in their desperation to escape. When I try to rise, a bearded man holds out a hand to help me.

'Get up, sister!' he says. 'Get up and run!'

I stand. I stare around the hall.

Where is Melzack? Where are my parents? I run towards a window where a few stragglers are climbing through.

Hundreds of disciples rush about. Fear in every face. Military helicopters hover low. Soldiers swarm towards the main building as some of Melzack's men begin to fire.

I am desperately scanning the crowd. Looking for my dad. Nothing. Nothing.

A megaphone blasts off from above: '**Put down your weapons!**'

Then a hand clutches at my arm. Tanya! The girl from the bunker. She's picked me out of the crowd. 'Where did they go?' I ask her. 'Did you see them?'

'Yes! The temple. Come with me.' She drags me towards a low-lying building.

As we sprint over I see a helicopter spinning above me; hear the tortured scream of an engine running out of control.

We crash-land hard on the tarmac. My face gets slammed against the back of a seat. Stars blitz my vision as pain bites. The rotors are fragged off in all directions and I feel my body wrenched downwards.

The engine whines louder. We're on a crazy slant. The soldiers are dazed but alive, piling out of the wreckage. Blood drips out of my nose.

'Secure the main hall!' Benson screams. Two seconds later he follows them out. Bullets smack into the metal. I tug on my seatbelt. Can't get it loose.

'Hey!' I yell. 'Hey!'

I'm alone in the chopper. Choking black fumes make me cough. I rip harder at the belt. It's super tight around my waist. My fingers cramp as I try to force the metal clip. It's jammed.

I try it again. Harder. Flames are licking round the roof. The smoke gets thicker. I rip at the metal with all my strength.

The clip flicks free. I scramble clear of the helicopter, my head still throbbing from the crash.

'Joe!' I hear this voice screaming my name. 'Joe! Over here!' It's her!

Joe runs towards me, dodging through the crowd. Blood streams from his nose, his T-shirt is caked in dirt. But I have never seen a happier sight in my life.

He falls into my arms and squeezes the air out of me. I hold him back, breathing his earthy scent, tighter than I have ever held anyone in my life, feeling a huge knot of emotion unravelling inside me.

'I'm sorry,' he gasps. 'I had to tell them. It's my dad ... he's ... '

The crashed helicopter explodes in a fury of sparks and flames. A fireball of hot air blasts towards us. The crowds scatter, heading for the woods, towards the gates – anywhere to get away.

'We're going to lose them,' Tanya urges. 'Come on!'

Joe and I pull apart and follow Tanya along the side of the building. As we go I tell Joe that 'Cora' is an imposter.

'No wonder she tried to get rid of me,' he says.

We get to a doorway. Locked. Tanya punches four numbers into a keypad. The door slides open. We step inside, and the door closes behind us with a swishing noise of compressed air. The chaos and noise of the outside world is suddenly muted.

We are in a place of deadly calm.

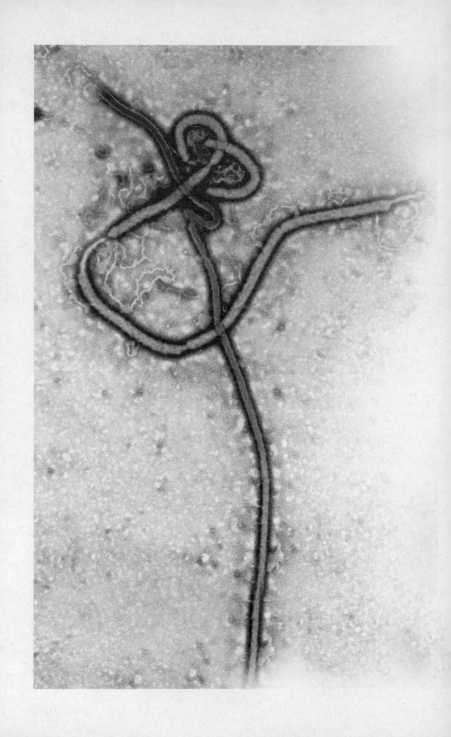

PART 13

MELTDOWN

Patrick Eden: He's delirious. He's broken the restraint! His eyes are rolling back ...

Police Command: The helicopter team is landing now.

Patrick Eden: His heart is failing. Breathing's out of control.

Audio transcript from helmet mic worn by Patrick Eden, UK Government bioweapons inspector following emergency call at SYMBARON lab, Hampshire.

We're in this kind of shrine. The walls are grey marble. There are ponds and goldfish and exotic plants. It feels weird, like a movie set.

'This way!' Tanya says. We go into a bigger room. There's a huge pile of burning papers in the middle of the floor.

'I expect he's getting rid of evidence,' Tanya says.

We duck behind a sofa.

'There!' Becca says. I stare through the smoke and flames. Just in time to see Melzack pushing Becca's mum and dad through a narrow doorway at the back of the building. Seconds later the Dog Poisoner and the girl that pretended to be Cora follow them in.

'Where does that lead?' Becca asks.

'There's a stairway inside,' the girl says. 'They say there are tunnels down there. Normally it's guarded.'

'An escape route,' Becca says. 'We have to follow.'

We dodge the pile of burning files and make our way to the doorway. In front of us are these spooky-looking stone steps, going down into blackness.

We can hear Melzack's voice echoing up, so we wait for a while. Then, quiet as we can, we follow them into the depths.

221 BECCA

The spiralling stone stairway goes incredibly deep. Maybe fifty metres or more. At the bottom we come out into a dark corridor cut out of the bare rock. Which way to go? Left or right?

There's a mildewy smell to the place and the air is thick and damp.

'Let's listen,' I whisper. 'Maybe we'll hear which way they went.'

We stay silent for a few seconds but there's no noise except our breathing. We walk towards a doorway just metres away and Joe pokes his head carefully around it to take a look.

'It's OK,' he whispers.

We step into another tunnel which looks like it might be an old mine. Dodgy wooden struts held together with rusty nails are holding up the roof. Water is dripping down the walls.

Then I detect voices. 'Shhh,' I tell them. 'I think I can hear my dad.'

'Come on!' Joe urges. 'Let's get a move on before we lose them.'

We hurry in the direction of the sound.

Suddenly Tanya gasps. She has bumped into a rusty metal stake leaning against the wall. Her hand shoots out to steady it.

Too late.

It falls to the floor with a sharp crash.

The clanging noise echoes down the tunnel. It seems to go on forever.

We stop dead. We're scanning ahead, looking for signs that Melzack is coming back.

After a couple of minutes, hearts thudding crazily, we creep forward again.

Five more minutes. Then we get to this place where another tunnel branches off. The dark outline of a pit is lurking ominously to our right, a hole cut deep into the rocky floor.

Suddenly lights flick on. Dazzling torches are in our eyes. Becca grabs my arm, her nails digging in. Melzack and 'Cora' come out of the shadows. They both have guns in their hands.

'You really don't ... know when to ... stop, do you?' Melzack wheezes.

'Let my parents go,' Becca begs him. 'You've got the virus, you don't need them.'

'I do ... need them,' he says. 'Your father is ... going to make sure ... that I have the vaccine ... for myself and ... my people. If he refuses ... I have your mother ... and I'm sure ... he won't want ... her to be hurt.'

Becca starts to say something but Melzack holds up his hand. He turns to 'Cora'.

'Kill them,' he says.

Then he limps away down the tunnel.

'Cora' watches Melzack as he moves off. She pulls back the safety catch on her gun and her mouth narrows into this grim little slit which could almost be a smile.

'Sorry about this,' she tells us. Her tone is casual, as if she's apologising for some minor inconvenience.

Fear in its purest essence floods every cell of my body.

'You're first,' she tells Tanya. Tanya stumbles back, her whole body shaking as she stares wide-eyed at the gun.

'Please,' Tanya whispers. She puts her hands together in a desperate symbol of prayer, 'I beg you ... don't ... '

The gun erupts in a flash of vicious power. Tanya is thrown backwards, her head disintegrating in a plume of red and grey matter. A scream of agony rises inside me. I swallow it back, gulping air. I grab at Joe. He puts his arm around me.

'Now you,' 'Cora' tells Joe. 'But I have one question first. How did they make you crack? What did they do to you that made you betray your girlfriend?'

'Stick it!' Joe tells her.

'Cora' pistol-whips him on the cheek. A lightning blow which sends him flying backwards, away from me. 'I asked you a question,' she repeats.

'And I said, *stick it*,' he says. His eyes are glittering with rage.

'All right,' 'Cora' snaps. 'I will.'

She raises the pistol to the centre of Joe's forehead.

Becca leaps in. Snatches at the gun. A shot smashes into the rocky roof. Chunks of stone zap everywhere. I rush at the girl. No plan. Just total aggression and flying fists. I get one in. Right on the killer's cheekbone.

For a second she's stunned. Then she shakes herself out of it – lashes out with her left hand.

'Help me! Hold the gun!' Becca staggers back under a blow. I reach for the weapon. Then the girl spins, an expert martial-arts move. She kicks me, right in the ribs. I hit the floor. Pain raging.

I see Becca go down; a judo throw has floored her.

Blood floods into my mouth as I spring back, crushing my fist into the back of the killer's neck. I grab her hair and pull her head back hard. Becca wrestles with the gun.

'Cora' is incredibly strong. Fingers gouge my eye. I scream in agony. But I don't stop hitting her.

The gun falls to the rocky floor. I kick it away. The tussle gets dirty. The killer bites Becca on the arm. Becca screams, pulls back.

I rush forward, smashing into her with both arms out-stretched. She trips back. To the edge of the pit. Her arms flail. She tries to balance. I snatch at her and miss. Then she falls with a strangled scream.

A split second later we hear the sickening thud as her body hits the bottom.

For a few long seconds the only sound is the rasp of our breathing. I feel my body tuning in to the pain of the fight.

'You OK?' I ask Joe. He nods. We step to the pit. I shine the torch downwards.

Ten feet below our position we see 'Cora', crashed out unconscious on the rocky ground.

'Do you think she's … ?' Joe asks.

'No. She's breathing.'

'Who *is* she? I mean who is she for real?'

'I have no idea.' I shake my head. 'A monster. Radicalised somehow, brainwashed by Melzack maybe.'

We turn back to Tanya. Her head is a horror show of bloodied tissue and shattered bone.

'I'm sorry,' I whisper to her. 'So sorry.' I turn away, retching as tears stream down my cheeks. I feel Joe's hand on my shoulder.

'Come here,' he says. His voice is thin, wavering. I turn towards him and he folds me in his arms for a few precious moments of contact. Then we step away from Tanya and head swiftly down the tunnel. My heart is filled with this terrible ocean of shock. Tanya is dead. And all she was trying to do was help us.

We set off and soon see Melzack's torch flickering in the distance – I can breathe again. We haven't lost them. My parents might still be saved.

We follow for a few minutes. My whole body is aching from the fight. I can feel my gouged eye beginning to swell right up.

Then the torchlight stops. At the same time a strange green glow begins to fill the tunnel. Daylight is coming in from above. The group moves out of sight and a little while later we hear the sound of Melzack ranting at Becca's mum and dad.

'Climb faster!' he goes. 'Come on!'

We hear Becca's mum sobbing. Then a metal clunking, then all goes quiet.

We move ahead, then look up into a circular shaft. A ladder is bolted into its wall.

'Me first,' I tell Becca.

We climb hand over hand, as quiet as we can. Up the steel rungs. Heading for that ring of green light. I'm thinking we should have picked up the gun, brought it with us.

We come out into woods and duck for cover. Melzack and the others are a short distance off, next to a small building, which I kind of recognise.

Then I see the two yellow Toyotas.

227 BECCA

My parents are pushed into the back seat of one of the cars. I lurch forward but Joe holds me back.

'You want to get shot?' he hisses. 'Let them go and we can follow them in the other one.'

Melzack and the Dog Poisoner look back towards the tunnel entrance. 'Where is she? We can't leave without her,' Melzack says.

They're wondering about 'Cora'. Then comes the noise of troops shouting nearby. I see movement through the trees.

Melzack and the Dog Poisoner start to argue, in low urgent tones. 'She can look after herself; use the motorbike,' I hear the Dog Poisoner say. He gestures to a bike lurking in the back of the garage.

Melzack looks reluctant, but the Dog Poisoner pushes him into the front passenger seat of the vehicle. Melzack takes a last regretful look at the tunnel entrance before he finally pulls the car door closed.

They power away at high speed and we sprint for the second car. Joe turns the key. The engine fires up with an animal snarl.

Left foot down. First gear select. Clutch up and we are off and I have 200 brake horsepower at my command. And despite the mayhem and the stress I can't help getting this massive surge because this machine is one *monster* bit of kit.

And it takes off faster than anything I have ever driven before. And six throbbing heartbeats after I've put my foot down we are already doing sixty miles per hour.

My damaged eye is now giving me just blurry images and a whole truckload of searing pain.

'The trees, Joe, careful of the **trees!**'

I fishtail the Toyota round a tight bend in the track. We miss this massive tree by about three inches. We're smashing through puddles. Mud is flying everywhere, stones are kicking up like bullets against the underside of the chassis.

But we're gaining on them. I'm going twice his speed. Branches whip against the screen.

229 BECCA

A wall is coming up fast. Then I see a gap with two guards and a barrier.

Melzack's car heads for the exit. It's got a wooden pole across it but the car smashes right through it like it isn't there. The guards leap for their lives. Joe follows, then we're out of the mission centre, in a small country lane, Melzack's vehicle accelerating at incredible speed.

'Come on baby,' Joe is whispering. He's talking to the car like it's a person.

We gain on Melzack. There's a lorry full of cattle ahead. A blind bend coming up.

Melzack's car pulls out to the right and overtakes the truck. He's taking incredible risks and he's got Mum and Dad on board. If there's anything coming the other way it'll be a head-on collision.

'Joe, don't do it!'

The engine roars as Joe puts his foot down. We fly around the corner with the wheels screaming, the hedge whizzing past in this incredible blur.

I take a quick glance out of the back window. No one's following. There's no flash of blue lights to say the security services are on Melzack's tail.

'It's down to us,' Joe says. 'If we don't catch him, no one will.'

He glances at me. I gasp as I see his eye is now swollen to the size of an egg.

I clutch on to the grab bars in front of me, my knuckles white.

The Toyota eats up the tarmac like some raging beast. I'm doing 110 miles per hour down this narrow lane and I feel totally in control.

'What are we going to *do* if we do catch them?' Becca asks, definite hysteria in her voice.

'Don't ask me,' I tell her. 'I'm making this up as I go along!'

I snatch a look at her. And I'm just so happy that all that blood on her shirt belongs to someone else.

A bridge sign flashes past. I remember it from before. It goes over a canal.

'We could ram them off the road,' I tell Becca. 'Sideswipe them a bit.'

'Don't forget that's my parents on board,' she snaps. 'Do *try* and bear that in mind when you're doing all this ramming and sideswiping.'

The steering wheel responds to my slightest touch. I feel like I'm a part of the machine. Like the cogs and propshafts and cylinders and sparks are gradually working their way into me. We're one and the same being.

231 BECCA

Melzack's car exits the road, making a lightning-fast turn to the left. It rockets across an area of grassland and drives flat out towards some bushes at the far end.

'I know what he's doing,' Joe says. 'He's going to drive along the towpath.'

'Towpath? What towpath? I can't even see a canal!'

'Down here!' Joe says. He swings the steering wheel hard and suddenly I can see water glistening darkly as we shoot down this steep embankment. We're on this crazy angle but two seconds later we crunch down on to the bottom of the slope and we're on a path alongside the canal.

'He thought he'd trick me then,' Joe says with a laugh. Then he shouts, 'Dream on, loser!'

I risk a glance at the speedometer. We are doing sixty miles per hour down this towpath. Feels all right. I press harder on the accelerator.

Becca doesn't seem to be enjoying the ride. 'This is *crazy!*' she screams.

'Relax!' I tell her.

'There's a fisherman ahead!'

'Yeah. I see him,' I tell her. 'I reckon he'll get out of the way.'

Melzack's vehicle doesn't even slow a fraction.

The fisherman jumps back into a ditch as it blasts past him. He's shaking his fist and shouting fit to bust as Melzack's car totals his gear and his seat with a nasty splat of plastic and wood.

Something flies up and smashes against our windscreen. The corner glazes up with a series of cracks.

There's a bridge ahead. A road going over. In the shadows beneath it I see a classy splash of colour. I slow down just a tiny bit. Just a few hundred revs. Just to take a little peek with my good eye. 'Nice tag!'

'I don't believe this!' Becca rages. 'We're trying to save my parents' lives and stop this maniac basically setting off world war three and you're actually *slowing down* to admire some graffiti!'

We pass a long line of narrowboats. We're hanging right on Melzack's tail.

Then I see a tunnel. 'Joe! It's a dead end!'

'I don't think so,' he says. 'If he puts his foot down he can get up that slope.'

I see the incline going up the side. There's a bit without trees and I know straight away what Joe is thinking.

Two seconds later Melzack's driver has taken the slope at full velocity, the car tilting like crazy, the wheels spinning as he climbs over the lip and disappears into the forest above.

'Nice move,' Joe says. 'He's good this guy.'

Joe doesn't even touch the brakes. Just drives straight at the slope and it's like we're going up the type of take-off ramp that those crazy motorbike stunt kids use to get airborne.

'Come on! Come on!' Joe is urging the car on like it's a horse or a husky or something.

I grit my teeth so hard my jaw feels like it's going to snap. We lurch up and over the lip with a massive **bump**.

'All right!' Joe yells.

We're out of the canal trap and into an open field. Some ponies are stampeding around, frightened by our engine noise. We blast through a gap, get back on a road. Suddenly I see Melzack's window glide down. Something metallic and black pokes out.

'Watch out!' Becca screams as the window on her side shatters into hundreds of pieces, tiny fragments of glass zapping all over the place.

Another gun flash. The front wheel explodes. The car judders as bits of tyre fly into the air.

Melzack's vehicle accelerates away.

'Don't lose them!' Becca cries. 'Keep going, Joe, please!'

We're driving on the rim. I'm squinting through the windscreen with my one good eye. Metal grinding against the tarmac. The car is filling with the stench of burning rubber and hot steel. Then I see the level crossing ahead.

'The barrier's coming down!' she yells. I see the flashing red lights. Hear the ringing of the warning bell. Melzack's car races on, gets there in the nick of time, just passing through before the barrier falls.

We're stuck for nearly a minute as an express train thunders past.

Then we come to a crossroads.

And they've disappeared.

'I don't believe it!' Joe says bitterly. 'All for the sake of one lousy tyre!'

'There's no way we're going to find them now,' I say.

We are silent for a few moments. And the stark reality of it slams into me in this crushing sense of hopelessness. My parents are lost. In the hands of a psychopath – a man who will stop at nothing to achieve his sick dreams of destruction.

I place my hand on Joe's. He grips me back as our fingers intertwine. 'You did your best, Joe. No one could have done more.'

'I'm sorry,' he tells me. He looks at me with his one good eye. I want to hold him. I need to hold him.

'Unless … ' I say. And this stupid little ember of hope flares into life.

'Unless what?' Joe asks.

'Unless we can work out where he's going.'

Joe looks at me like I'm crazy. He gestures at the different ways Melzack could have taken my parents.

'How would we do that?' he asks scathingly. 'Magic?'

'No. Logic.' I tell him. 'That's what Dad always told me. There's no mystery that can't be solved by using logic.'

'He has to be heading somewhere specific,' Becca says.

'Maybe he's got a safe house?' I suggest.

'Perhaps,' she says doubtfully. 'But it's not really enough for him to go to ground in this country. He's responsible for murder. His cult members have shot down an army helicopter.'

'Yeah. It's true, they'd find him pretty fast.'

'So ... he has to flee the country,' she says. 'He has to get across the channel somehow and lose himself, in Europe, or Africa.'

'Hmmm. It's possible.'

'How would he get out of the country?'

'Fast boat?' I suggest. I'm starting to get a bit more interested in her idea.

At that moment a throbbing noise cuts through the conversation. Seconds later a little plane flies overhead. Its flaps are down and the engine note decreases as it wobbles in the evening breeze.

'It's coming in to land,' I say. 'Must be an airfield over there somewhere.'

'That's it!' she says.

I fire up the engine and put the car into gear.

'Follow that plane, Joe!' she says. 'Whatever happens, don't lose it.'

We take off down the lane, the one closest to the direction the plane is taking. Thirty miles per hour. Forty. The scraping, grinding mayhem from the front of the car is enough to set my teeth on edge.

'Left here, Joe!' I tell him. It sounds like we are gouging a channel the depth of the Grand Canyon into the tarmac as we go.

The light aircraft is still in view, coming down to land about half a mile from our position. Then I see flames licking around the bonnet. 'We're on fire!' I tell Joe.

'Yeah, we are,' he says nonchalantly. 'That happens to loads of rally cars. Those drivers don't get too phased by it so I won't either.'

The aircraft drifts down behind a row of trees. I find myself praying that my theory about Melzack fleeing the country is correct. And if he really is at the airfield, will we be in time to stop him?

I steal a look at Joe. It's a miracle how calm he's kept throughout this whole thing. And a miracle he's stuck with me. He looks amazingly handsome right now, and less like a boy. More like ...

'Hey, Joe,' I tell him softly. 'Thanks for everything you're doing for me.'

'That's OK,' he says.

We see a sign: WEST HAMPTON AIRFIELD. Joe drives in.

We're into the airfield. A small clubhouse ahead. I drive through a car park, gravel spitting in all directions. The engine's well on fire. Three men start shouting. They're running after us.

'There's the runway!' Becca yells.

I drive towards it. A thin strip of tarmac in the middle of a big grass field. The plane we've been following is just turning off it.

'There he is!' Becca shouts. She points to the right.

I see Melzack's motor. It's parked outside a hangar. A control tower nearby. There's a small aeroplane next to it and the prop is already running. There's a pilot in the hot seat.

'They're in the back!' she yells. I see her parents in the rear of the plane.

Melzack and the Dog Poisoner are climbing in beside them. They look in our direction as we speed towards them. We must look a crazy sight, with one side of the car scraping along the ground. Flames leaping out of the front.

The aircraft door closes. The plane pulls away, picking up speed.

'Faster!' Becca screams.

I ram my foot down on the accelerator. The Toyota gives us a last surge of power.

The aircraft starts to turn towards the runway. The engine roaring as the prop spins.

'Here we go,' I tell Becca. 'You might want to keep your head down.'

Joe slams right into the front of the airplane. Rams it at about fifty miles per hour.

There's a horrendous bang. The windscreen shatters. Something hits me hard on the temple. We spin through a quarter turn. The propeller cuts through the roof just behind us in a series of rapid-fire impacts. Splinters of carbon fibre spray about the car's interior as I cradle my head in my hands.

'Get out!' Joe shouts.

I stagger from the car. I am choking deep in my lungs. The smoke is thicker with every second. The noxious smell of burning plastic fills the air.

'Mum! Dad!'

I race towards the rear of the aircraft. Flames are growing at the front. The interior is swirling with fumes. People are arriving from the clubhouse. Someone cries 'Get the fire extinguishers!'

The pilot and the Dog Poisoner emerge from the smoke. Someone shouts, 'They've got a gun!' The two men run over to a car that has just pulled up, put the weapon to the driver's head and drag her out. Then they drive away at high speed.

'Rebecca!' Mum's voice cuts through the shouts, the crackle of flames.

She's standing on the other side of the shattered plane, having scrambled free of the wreckage. She's safe! I want to run to her, but there's no time. I turn back to the aircraft door that is closest to me. I see a shape moving inside.

Dad!

I run to Becca. We open the aircraft door. I take one hand. She takes the other. We pull like mad. Drag the spluttering figure out. Two of the men from the clubhouse join in, helping us to get him into the clear air of the hangar.

He lies there, chest heaving, his face blackened with smoke. Half conscious and moaning.

'It's Melzack!' Becca spits the name in disgust.

We just saved the one man we didn't want to.

'We can always drag him back in there,' I tell her.

'Dad? Dad!' Becca calls. All we can see is smoke.

One of the flying-club men is giving me an evil look. He's an elderly bloke with a moustache, but he looks strong.

'You were the driver!' he snarls. He grabs me hard, forcing me down on to my knees. 'Call the police, Nigel!'

'They'll be here in ten minutes!' a voice shouts through the smoke. 'Fire brigade as well.'

Then a bent-up figure comes through the smoke. It's Becca's dad! And he's got the case with him, the one carrying the virus.

'Dad!' Rebecca runs across the hangar and hugs her dad like crazy. Then her mum comes over and all three of them are hugging and crying and ...

I'm so happy for her. I really am.

241 BECCA

This has to be the strangest family group hug in history. Here with this hornets' nest swarming out around us.

I move towards Joe. The flying-club man still has him in a vicious grip.

'Are you trying to break his arm?' I ask him.

'He should have thought about that before he came in here trying to trash the place,' he says. 'What's all this about, anyway?'

Joe grunts in pain.

'Something to do with drugs probably,' the older man next to him says. 'Rival gangs – smuggling across the Channel.'

'Are you all right?' I ask Joe. I kneel beside him and I just wish the man would let go so I could give him a long hug.

'Yeah. Hundred per cent,' he tells me with a smile. 'Never been better.'

'You were in that car as well,' one of the club people suddenly points a finger in my direction. 'You're a part of this.'

He steps towards me.

'That's the real criminal.' I turn to point to Melzack but a new wall of thick smoke has filled the hangar and he cannot be seen. I hear the sound of a scuffle, a blow.

Then the smoke drifts away and Melzack is standing there, his arm around Dad's neck, a gun aimed at his temple. Mum is unconscious on the floor.

The case containing the virus is in Dad's hand.

The shouts dry up as everyone in the hangar sees what's happening. The only noise is the sound of the aircraft crackling as it burns.

'I need ... a plane,' Melzack grunts towards us. His voice is hoarse but he can still be understood. 'Someone has ... to fly us out ... of here.'

'You're not going anywhere!' the flying-club man shouts.

He lets go of me and takes a few determined steps towards Melzack.

'No!' Becca screams. The gun fires. The old man jerks backwards and lies twitching on the concrete floor, a stream of blood pumping from his neck.

'A plane ... now!' Melzack says. But the other members of the flying club have turned and run.

Melzack's face contorts. He starts to drag Becca's dad backwards, towards the stairs that lead up to the control tower.

'Let him go!' Becca yells.

Becca sprints after them. Reaches the bottom of the stairwell.

A second bullet rips through the air. Becca ducks as it ricochets off the wall beside her.

'Stay back, Rebecca!' her dad calls. I run to Becca's side.

Melzack lets off two more shots. Pain rages down my arm.

Joe stumbles back. I catch his weight, we smash against a wall. I lower him to the floor. Blood wells from dozens of small puncture wounds along his arm and shoulder.

'I'm OK,' he gasps. 'I think.'

He stares at the injuries, eyes rolling wide.

'Shrapnel,' he hisses through gritted teeth. 'Won't kill me ...'

The sound of a scuffle erupts from above. I hear Dad grunt as he takes a blow.

'Go to him!' Joe says.

'Dad!' I take the steps at a sprint.

The stairwell is dark. At the top, all I can see is a confusion of flailing arms as two shadowy figures trade blows.

I leap on to Melzack's back, beat at his head with my fist. Melzack cries out. The gun erupts. Dad jerks sideways, his calf gushing blood.

Melzack throws me off. Snatches the case. I lunge for the weapon, get a hand on it as he bodycharges me. We crash into the empty control room. The gun goes spinning. I dive forward and grab it, springing to my feet. I hear distant sirens. The police are almost here.

Melzack pulls the virus flask from the case. His fingers shake as he twists at the cap.

'Put it down,' I tell him. The gun is aimed directly at his heart.

Melzack holds up the vial, taunting me as he spins the lid another turn.

'The police will ... breathe it ... as they come in ... take the virus ... out into the world ... the infection will spread ... thousands will still die ... perhaps millions.'

His eyes glitter with a manic internal fire.

'Think about your daughter,' I say. 'Do you really believe

this is what she would have wanted?'

I hear the sound of a motorbike pulling up outside. Melzack hears it too and glances out of the window. His expression softens and he lowers the vial.

'You ask what ... my daughter would ... have thought?' he smiles.

Footsteps are running up the stairs. The door swings open.

'Why don't you ... ask her yourself?'

'Cora' is standing in the doorway, a gun in her hand. Her face is bloodied and swollen.

'Hello Rebecca,' she says. Her gun explodes, blitzing my shoulder as a bullet sears through my flesh. I crash to the floor, dropping the gun. My body is torn up with pain.

'Cora' is Melzack's *daughter*?

The room turns, blurring as my vision swims. The floor is slick with blood. My blood. I get a sudden vision of those eyes in the undergrowth – the ones on the video. Those haunting eyes.

Phoenix.

The two figures loom above, staring down at me.

'Meet Phoenix,' Melzack says. He puts his arm around her and kisses the top of her head.

Melzack's daughter. I should have worked it out. No one but family could be so utterly in tune with Melzack's plans.

If anyone was going to be radicalised of course it would be her. But ...

'The biography ... ' I gasp. 'It says you died of Ebola.'

'No it doesn't,' she replies. 'It says I got a lethal dose of Ebola. It doesn't actually say I died.'

'But the river ... ? You were swept ... ?'

'The hospital ran out of morphine. I couldn't take the pain so I went to the river and threw myself in. I woke up in a hut two days later, ten miles downstream.'

Phoenix's face swims in and out of focus as waves of

agony engulf me.

'A hunter and his family had found me,' she continues. 'Washed up on a sandbank. Somehow my immune system had got me through the worst of the Ebola but half of the muscles in my body were destroyed.'

She raises her left hand, stroking her frozen face with her fingers.

'Everyone thought I was dead. I saw a newspaper where an American general called me a "casualty of war",' she says. 'That was when I decided to go undercover and fight back. Teach them what a "casualty of war" really is.'

My eyes flicker to Melzack. His fingers are still wrapped around the neck of the vial.

'My girl's ... a survivor,' Melzack says proudly. 'She trekked ... for a thousand miles ... across Africa ... living ... with local villagers ... learning to hunt and shoot.'

'And kill,' his daughter adds.

Sirens rage at the top end of the runway. Melzack hands the vial to Phoenix.

'Run!' he urges her. 'Dark Heart can still happen if you escape.'

Phoenix embraces her father.

'The schools ... ?' I whisper. 'Whose idea?'

'Mine,' Phoenix says proudly.

I get a sudden premonition of the thousands of children who will die in agony if Dark Heart works. The millions who will lose their lives if the virus spreads. And that's what gives me the strength to pick up the gun. And aim it straight at Phoenix's head.

I know she might drop the vial if she falls. But I can't let her escape from this place.

'You haven't got the nerve,' she laughs.

I am staring right into her eyes.

My finger tightens on the trigger.

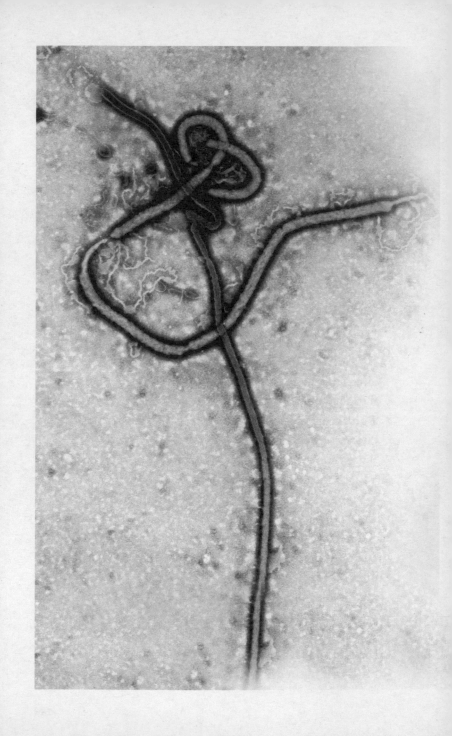

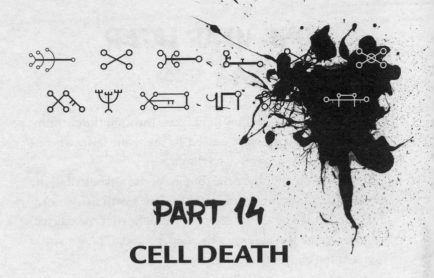

PART 14

CELL DEATH

Patrick Eden: He's gone into shutdown. Not responding. The flames are getting closer (coughs). Thicker ...

Police Command: Smoke coming from the air vents. Fire brigade attending in two minutes. Get out, Patrick! Now!

Patrick Eden: It's over for Simon ... it's over.

Audio transcript from helmet mic worn by Patrick Eden, UK Government bioweapons inspector following emergency call at SYMBARON lab, Hampshire.

ONE YEAR LATER
244 BECCA

Birdsong wakes me. Mellow light filters through the curtains.

I dress myself and walk out on to the front lawn where I stretch and yawn a greeting to the day.

The sun is already above the roofline of the old barn and the air has that innocent, fresh feel that comes with early morning. You can tell by the intensity of the light that the day will be warm once the sun gets the upper hand. There's still a touch of fog clinging to the ground.

Arcturus is waiting in the shadows of the stall. I swing the door open and step towards him, running my hand down his neck and murmuring a few soft words of greeting. He nuzzles my hand, looking for a treat. Half an apple slips into my palm and he crunches it appreciatively as I lead him out into the yard.

I slip the other half of the apple to Andromeda, the horse my mother bought shortly after she came back to live with us again. She hasn't ridden him yet and I am not sure she ever will. Her demons are still there.

I climb on to Arcturus's back with a single smooth movement, a thrill of anticipation running through me. Apart from anything I want to prove to myself that my shoulder is finally healed.

'Come on boy. Let's have some fun.'

I gently kick my heels. Arcturus turns a circle. He's a bit confused. He doesn't quite know how to act. I've never ridden him bareback before. I snatch at his mane to stop myself being thrown off backwards. I am laughing. His eyes are rolling back, as if to ask me *are you serious?*

I'm serious, my loyal horse. We do a couple of gentle circuits of the garden, warming up for twenty minutes. Then I dig my heels in.

'Yaaargh!'

Arcturus shoots ahead. The surge of power is instant and strong, filled with the joy of movement, with the freedom of being out in a beautiful fresh summer morning. It's almost like he's decided, *'All right. If that's the way you want to play it!'* I turn him towards the copse. We blaze an anarchic trail of hoof prints right across the croquet lawn.

We enter the woods. Arcturus finds a bit more strength from within. He picks up yet more speed.

I urge him on. Whippy little branches flick against my head. I make my profile low. Hugging my noble horse tight and placing my cheek against his neck. I can feel the heat radiating from his body. The rhythmic surge of muscle. The sweet smell of sweat as he gets into his pace.

Arcturus is loving this. And so am I. But it will take more than a horse ride to stop living and reliving the events of last year. We pass the tree ...

... where all of this began.

The bell blasts off. One of those old fashioned metal ones that's so loud it makes your teeth hurt. It's about an arm's length from my bunk. I wrap the pillow round my head but nothing can keep that jangling out of my ears. It's 7 a.m.

Me and the three lads sharing my cell drag ourselves into the corridor. We're bleary-eyed. Watchful for trouble. The gangs in here are vicious if you cross them.

Another happy day in paradise. Otherwise known as Feltham Young Offenders Institution.

We line up. Pass through the guard inspection. One corridor later we're entering the canteen where the smell of bacon and eggs fills the air.

I grab a plate. Get my share. I keep my eyes down; keep my head down.

There was a time, not long ago according to some of the stories, when Feltham was a real mess. An average of two stabbings a week. Loads of lads locked up in solitary. Drugs in every cell. The guards using batons on legs and arms.

Now it's been 'cleaned up' and it's an easier ride for loners like me. The drugs are still here if you go looking for them, but the violence is a bit more under control. I got pressured to join a couple of gangs but I stood my ground.

It's the smell that gets me. The mix of sweat, toilet cleaner and old cooking grease.

When I get out of here I'm going to shower for a week.

The memory of Dad hanging from the tree. My desperate fight to cut him down. The deep sound of bone impacting wood as his head hit the tree root. I relive those moments every day.

But the way the story ended haunts me harder: my finger tightening on the trigger. Phoenix's arrogant black eyes drilling into me. Squeezing to the point of ... explosion.

The shot came from the hangar. Through the window of the control tower. A police sniper fired a bullet with incredible precision into the centre of Phoenix's forehead. A split second later the same projectile passed through the shattered remains of her skull and killed her father.

The two of them hit the floor simultaneously.

The sound of a helicopter was approaching. I heard faraway footsteps running up the stairs.

Joe's voice: 'Becca!' I turned for the door.

Then the loss of blood overwhelmed me and the world went black.

The last thing I remember was Joe cradling me in his arms.

A year has gone by. But the jagged dreams are still with me.

The fight I could hear kicking off in the control tower. The girl we knew as Cora rushing past. The pain from the shrapnel wounds as I got to my feet.

I staggered up the stairs, stepping over Becca's dad who looked injured but OK. Through the door of the control tower I could see Becca.

Melzack and the girl were lying motionless on the floor. Becca was bleeding heavily from the shoulder, crashed on the ground. I sat beside her and took her head in my hands.

Four figures came in; Benson's men in biosuits, the anti-terrorism team from the helicopter. I was ripped away, pulled down the stairs and thrown in the back of a police van.

And for the next three days I had no idea if Becca was dead or alive.

I woke up in hell; otherwise known as a level-4 biohazard isolation room at Porton Down Defence Science and Technology Laboratory in Wiltshire.

Benson's team had to play it safe, keep me apart from the rest of the world until they could be sure I hadn't been exposed to the virus.

My shoulder got reconstructive surgery, a patch-up job which left me biting the pillow with agony as the bone and tissue began to heal.

Finally, sixteen days later, weighing a stone less than when I went in and weak as a kitten, I was released for debriefing with the team from Defence HQ.

After six hours of questioning I was shown into a small room where Mum and Dad were waiting. Dad was limping from his leg wound but otherwise OK. Holding them in my arms was the moment I finally believed the nightmare might be coming to an end.

The whole thing was covered up. No press people have, so far, found out the truth about Melzack's plan. The government took great pains to spin a concocted story to the press, downplaying the events at the airfield and describing it as an attempted plane-jacking gone wrong. The virus flask was spirited away by Benson's men to an unknown destination.

Some journalists were suspicious. But none have guessed the truth. So the government has moved on. Walked away.

Lie. Kill. Walk away. That was the expression Dad used to describe the way these agencies act.

But have I really been any better? During the whole affair I certainly lied, and I was ready to kill. Only by the slightest fraction of a second was it that the sniper's bullet – and not mine – killed Melzack and his daughter.

Ready to kill.

I think about that a lot. Would I really have done it? Ended another human life? Shot Phoenix in cold blood?

That is why the walking away part is something I cannot do; my conscience won't let me. Because when I jolt awake, in the small hours of the morning, I ask myself this question: would I really have pulled that trigger?

And I'm not sure I can live with the answer.

249 JOE

A lot of trade-offs were done behind the scenes once Becca recovered.

I was offered a deal by Benson. Keep quiet about my involvement with Becca and her dad and the fake murder video showing me killing the Dog Poisoner would never be mentioned again. But I got ten months in Feltham on two counts: the incident when Becca and I took the Range Rover, and totalling the aeroplane and the Toyota at the airfield.

As much as anything I think it was a warning to keep my mouth shut.

Dad got his sentence for the illegal diesel reduced on appeal. He'll be home in a year if all goes well. He's looking fit after his heart op. I've been let out a couple of times to see him. He's still going to back me on the rally driving thing, so I haven't given up on that.

I've made some good mates inside. There are a few of the 'scum' that Derek warned me about, but most of the lads are all right. We get twelve hours of 'education' every week. I pass the time in the library. Reading about science. Learning about her world. The world of the girl I used to think of as Little Miss E.

Becca.

I'm released in three days. Pauline's going to meet me. But I'm wondering if Becca will be there as well. Waiting outside. I did write to her to let her know when I was coming out.

Stupid to even think it really. She's probably forgotten all about me.

Melzack and his daughter were buried in an unmarked grave in a secret location. The government were desperate to avoid their last resting place becoming some sort of warped shrine.

I think about Phoenix a lot. Wonder at the evil that had been unlocked inside her.

Radicalisation. In the most extreme form.

And that video still haunts me. Her eyes in the darkness of the African bush.

It provokes more questions inside me. I wonder how I would have reacted if that atrocity had happened to me. If I had been described as a 'casualty of war'.

Would I have been like her? Ready to kill thousands in revenge? If it had been *my* mother shot in front of me with the words:

'Waste her.'

I don't know the answer. Perhaps I don't want to know.

Shortly after the events at the airfield, Marcus Benson was sacked from his position at the MOD – a result of his mishandling of the whole affair. Recently Dad told me he was given a 'hardship' posting as a lowly military attaché at the British Embassy in Mongolia.

Melzack's henchman – the man Joe called the Dog Poisoner – escaped. Rumour has it he is in the Horn of Africa, building a new cult centre in one of the region's failed states. It seems he is styling himself as Melzack's rightful heir.

One question often runs through my mind: has the Dog Poisoner still got Dad's notebook? Is he even now working with a team of scientists to bring new bioweapons to life? Or was the notebook destroyed in the army raid on Melzack's mission centre?

I guess we won't know for sure – unless a new wave of

devastating viruses is suddenly unleashed on an unsuspecting world.

I live in fear of that.

Dad has cut all his ties with Defence HQ. He works for the United Nations on their inspection teams now, travelling to the war-torn corners of the planet. He is still watched by the security services, still the guardian of a hundred secrets they do not want to be known.

Once you have become a whistle-blower, you are never trusted again. Even if what you revealed was the truth.

Mum has sold her narrowboat and moved back in with us. She is healing, slowly, but she struggles to connect with me and with Dad, no matter how much we try. One day I asked her what had made her want to come back. She told me the long incarceration inside the vault had taken her to the edge and caused her to re-evaluate everything.

'It was my long dark night of the soul,' she told me. 'I was so close to death it helped me to see things in a different way. I realised I was ready to return to you all, that the years on my own had to end.'

So she is here. But days go by when we hardly speak. We have become a family again, but not like it was before.

The adrenaline rush is over. I feel Arcturus slowing as we reach the hedge that marks the end of the woods. We turn, riding more sedately back towards the house, weaving through the trees.

Then I see another horse, coming through the woods. At first the horse and rider are obscured by the forest. I find myself wondering who on earth it can be. The neighbouring farmer? Someone lost on a country ride? Then they emerge into a glade where they are illuminated by a brilliant wash of sunlight.

It's Mum. Riding Andromeda! At first I am just amazed. Then my heart soars with pride. I know what a big step this is for her. I bring Arcturus alongside her.

'I thought we might go for a ride together,' she says with a smile.

We turn the horses, riding side by side, heading for the open fields.

I wake up in Feltham for the very last time. There's a nice day out there by the looks of it. Blue sky through the bars.

Becca never replied to my letter. I have no idea if I will ever see her again.

I take a good look around while I'm waiting for midday. Just for the memories. Because I tell you one thing. I'm not coming back to Feltham Young Offenders Institution. No sir. Once I walk out that door that's it for me. Goodbye to the jangling bells. Goodbye to the shiny tiles and the flickering fluorescent lights. Goodbye to the sarky guards. Goodbye to the treacle sponge that sticks to your teeth; the stink of 750 smelly lads who aren't allowed aerosol deodorant because they'll end up sniffing it.

Goodbye to the gangs that will pounce if they see the slightest weakness. Goodbye to some mates as well. See ya! I'm out of here.

I kick my heels in the library while I'm waiting for them to chuck me out. Say thanks to Andrea, the lady that runs it. She's been good to me. Got me all the books I asked for. Made me secret cups of tea when she wasn't really supposed to.

Then it's time to pack my little bag. Pass through the clanking doors. A nod from the guards.

Pauline is waiting in the office. It's nice to see her.

'How are you, Joe?' She holds me so tight I can hardly breathe.

I'll be living with her now while we wait for my dad to be released. It'll be all right, I reckon.

There's some papers to sign. Release forms and stuff. Then we're out of the front gates and I'm back in the real world. And it feels so good. To get that clean air inside me. And look out further than the wall in front of your nose. And feel you can go in any direction, not just the one the guards tell you to go in.

And to see Becca standing on the other side of the road.

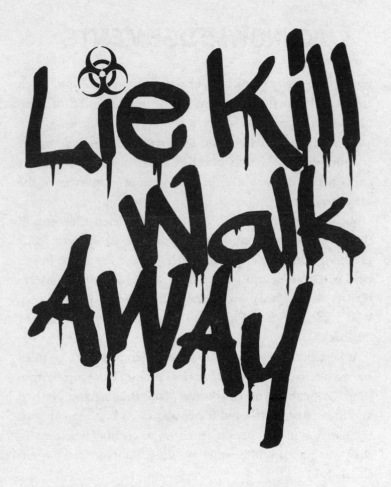

Want to read the alternative ending to *Lie Kill Walk Away*?
Visit **www.mattdickinson.com**

ACKNOWLEDGEMENTS

Phew! Once again I look back into the dim mists of time when this book began (eight years ago to be precise) and think how lucky I am to have had so much wonderful help.

My sons Tom, Ali, Greg and Dani were a constant source of encouragement. Thanks boys! Fi Dickinson, Steph Hunter and Bri English have also been long-time supporters of the idea and have helped to shape it in many ways.

Nicky Hetherington, Ellen Krajewski, Helen Cleaves and Bridget March were kind enough to organise student focus groups for the early drafts. My sincere thanks to all the pupils who participated and particularly to Becky Allen, Charlotte Hawley, Molly Jankowski, Jake Lillis, Ellie Longman-Rood, Will Luck, Rebekah Finch and Danny Riley for excellent feedback.

At Vertebrate Publishing 'Team Matt' continues to go from strength to strength, with first class backup from Jon Barton, John Coefield, Lorna Hargreaves, Jane Beagley and Nathan and Susie Ryder. If a publisher was rated by the quality of the pies and mushy peas it serves up to authors who pop in, then you guys would be stacking those Pulitzer prizes up on the shelves!

Well, you will be anyway. It's only a matter of time.

When the chips were down and deadlines loomed, Ruth Eastham happily read and corrected and advised on the story in the most wonderful ways. Thanks Ruth! You made the whole thing a lot more fun and a better book all round.

Finally, I want to acknowledge the role that the scientist and weapons expert David Kelly had in inspiring me to create this story. His life and (highly suspicious) death in 2003 was the flame that lit the blue touchpaper that became this book.

For any young readers who may not be familiar with David Kelly's story I urge you to google him right now and find out more. He was a decent man who sought only to tell the truth. Dark forces within the government of that time hounded him to his death and buried him beneath a pile of lies.

My anger at the way he was treated was how this book began.

ABOUT THE AUTHOR

Matt Dickinson is an award-winning writer and filmmaker with a passion for climbing and adventure. During his film-making career he has worked as a director/cameraman for National Geographic television, the Discovery Channel, the BBC and Channel 4. His film projects have taken him to Antarctica, Africa and the Himalaya, often in the company of the world's leading climbers and expeditioners. His most notable film success was *Summit Fever* in which Matt reached the summit of Everest via the treacherous north face. His book *The Death Zone* tells the true story of that ascent and has become a bestseller in many different countries.

Matt is currently patron of reading at Lady Manners School in Bakewell and continues to climb and explore. In January 2013 he summited Mount Aconcagua, which, at 6,965 metres, is the highest peak in the world outside the Himalaya. In 2016 he was back on Everest as writer in residence with Jagged Globe's South Col Expedition. Currently, he is planning an ascent of Denali in Alaska, one of the 'Seven Summits'.

Recently Matt has started writing fiction for teenage readers. His debut thriller series *Mortal Chaos* was well received by critics and readers alike. Matt has followed this up with *The Everest Files*, a dramatic and popular trilogy set on the world's highest mountain. *Lie Kill Walk Away* is his latest teen thriller. When he's not writing, Matt tours the UK, speaking at schools and colleges and inspiring a new generation of adventurers.

ALSO BY
MATT DICKINSON

Follow Ryan Hart's adventure in
The Everest Files books ...

The Everest Files.

A missing teenage climber. A trail of deadly clues.
Mystery on the world's highest peak.

North Face.

A deadly earthquake in the Himalaya. A climber trapped high
on Everest. An epic rescue attempt is about to begin.

Killer Storm.

A helicopter crash in the icefall. A white-out blizzard rolls in.
The scene is set for the ultimate Everest drama.

If you would like an author visit from Matt Dickinson for your
school or club, or if you just want to find out more about
The Everest Files, details can be found at
www.everestfiles.com